Peter sank back down. 'We're losing. We aren't well.'

'Are there still others? Are there Lost Boys?'

'Yes,' said Peter. 'But we need more help. That's why I came.'

'How can we help?'

Peter shrugged his shoulders. 'I don't know. I always come here to get help.'

'But if it isn't Hook,' said James, 'who is the enemy now?'

Peter took a deep breath and rubbed his side where the pain was. 'The Driller.'

# Neverland

**Toby Forward**

**Illustrated by John Talbot**

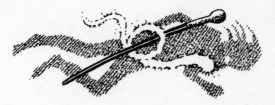

# S I M O N  &  S C H U S T E R

LONDON • SYDNEY • NEW YORK • TOKYO • SINGAPORE • TORONTO

Text copyright © 1989 Toby Forward
Illustrations copyright © 1989 John Talbot

First published in Great Britain in 1989
by Simon & Schuster Ltd

Published in paperback in 1990 by Simon & Schuster Young Books

Set in Baskerville 12/14pt
Printed and bound in Great Britain by Billing & Sons Ltd, Worcester

Simon & Schuster Young Books
Simon & Schuster Ltd
Wolsey House
Wolsey Road
Hemel Hempstead HP2 4SS

British Library Cataloguing in Publication Data available

ISBN 0 7500 0457 6

*To my brother,*
*John Forward*

# One

THE noise of the boy's crying woke James up. It was
a hot night, close with just a slight breeze that lifted the
curtain at his open window. The full moon threw light
into the room, slanting over the screwed-up face of the
boy sitting at the foot of James's bed.

'Boy,' said James. 'Why are you crying?'

'Not crying,' the boy answered. He scraped his bare
forearm over his wet eyes. Then he shook his head as
though it had been he, not James, who had just wakened
from sleep.

'Yes you were.'

'Not crying. I've got a cold.' This time he dragged his
arm over his nose and gave a loud, wet sniff. 'Funny,' he
said. 'I never get a cold.'

James reached out to the side of his bed and handed
him a box of tissues. The boy looked but did not take it.

'What's that?'

'Tissues. For your nose.'

The boy took the box and turned it over in his hands.
A tissue was dangling out, waiting to be pulled. He gave
another wet sniff.

'Blow,' said James.

The boy held the box up to his nose and blew into it. Then he couldn't find any way of wiping. James stared at him.

'It's no good,' said the boy and he threw the box on to the floor in a temper and dragged his arm over his nose again. James didn't want to pull the soggy tissue from the top of the box to show him so he left it alone.

'What are you doing here?'

'Don't know. Not well. Can't remember very well.' He let his head fall into his hands.

The room was very bright under the full moon and James sat up in bed and looked at the boy. They were about the same age, but the boy was slender and just a bit taller than James. James was stocky and powerful for his age. He wasn't fat but he looked as though he might be fat when he got older. The boy was tanned but underneath the colour there was no glow of health. He was right, he wasn't well. Still, James thought, he *was* crying when I woke up. I know he was, whatever he says. It was eerie having a strange boy sitting on his bed at, he looked at his clock radio by the bed, half past two in the morning. They were three floors up so he hadn't come in through the open window.

The road outside was quiet. When the boy wasn't sniffing James thought he could hear the tiny bell-like sound of the wind-chimes outside the front door. He had never heard it up in his bedroom before.

With his slim legs and bare arms the boy looked like an athlete or a gymnast. He was wearing a leotard or some sort of athletic costume with spider-web patterns on it. He lifted his head from his hands and stared around, confused.

'There's only one bed,' he said.

'Yes.'

'Where are the others?'

'In their own rooms.'

'This is their room.'

'It used to be. We split up last year. We've all got our own rooms now. Mum said we were getting too old to share.'

The boy nodded but didn't look as though he understood.

'Which one are you?' he asked.

It seemed a strange way to ask someone their name, but James answered. 'I'm James.' He thought it would be rude to ask straight out who his visitor was but now he felt that the boy's question had given him permission.

'Who are you?'

The boy didn't answer but sat up, fighting his illness and trying not to look too weak. He turned his head from side to side, letting James see him clearly in the moonlight.

'See?'

'Yes.'

'I'm back.'

'I don't know what you mean.'

'I've come back. Like I said.'

'But who are you?'

The breeze lifted the curtain even further away from the open window, curling it up like a beckoning hand, and the wind-chime stirred more loudly, floating its bell noise through the air like mocking laughter. The boy grimaced and put his hand to his side. James saw that he had reached down to clutch a dagger pushed through his belt.

'Peter,' he said, announcing himself with as much menace and dignity as he could muster in his weak state. 'I'm Peter, and I'm back.'

James shivered as the breeze touched his bare shoulders. Then the boy slumped back down again on the bed and looked very ill.

James didn't know what to do. He wasn't frightened. The boy looked too slender and weak to hurt him, even if he had got a dagger. But there was something about

him that was wrong and James couldn't work it out. He was nervous and this made him annoyed with the wind-chime. It was getting louder and now it was chiming all the time even though the breeze seemed to have drop-ped. The tinkling was jangling about inside his head so that he couldn't be sure any longer whether it was really there or whether he was dreaming it. Perhaps he was dreaming it all? He slipped out of bed and made his way towards the door. His sister would know what to do. She was two years older than he was.

At the door he turned and looked at Peter. The moon-light still fell across the bed, but instead of casting Peter's shadow away from him it drew it towards the window in quite the wrong direction, quite the opposite of where it should be. Although the boy was quite still, the shadow shimmered and flickered as though it tried to fly out of the window and up towards the moon. James frowned, turned the handle of the door and was gone.

Peter did not notice him leave, but as the door shut a small ball of light, about the size of a fist, rose up from behind a cupboard and floated towards Peter, making the tinkling noise that James had thought was from the wind-chimes. It hovered over Peter's slumped shoulders, ringing clearly.

'No,' he said to it after a moment. 'No.' Then, 'I'm not sure.'

It spoke to him again.

'I thought I knew who would be here, but I'm wrong. I don't know. I don't remember anything any more.'

The ball of light gave an agitated flutter and darted to the window, hovering there, waiting.

'Not yet. I'm too tired. It's taken it out of me, coming here. And besides, I don't think I can remember the way back.'

The chimes jangled again, not a sweet tinkling but a harsh, brassy clang. Peter shook his head. Then, as the door opened, the light darted away from the window and back behind the cupboard where it hid almost silently, listening.

'There he is,' said James.

A look of disbelief left his sister's face when she saw the boy. She had thought that James was teasing her, or having a nightmare. As she stepped into the room the shadow gave a terrific flick, then stopped, shivering and holding itself quiet, still falling in quite the wrong direction.

'Boy,' she said. 'Why are you crying?'

The boy looked up and shouted at her. 'I'm not crying, I tell you. Why don't you . . .?'

James's sister flinched as he shouted. Her face twisted as though he had hit her. The boy stopped.

'All right. That'll do,' said James. 'There's no need . . .'

'I'm back,' said the boy to James's sister.

'Yes,' she said. 'I've been waiting for you.'

The bells clanged angrily behind the cupboard and the ball of light rose up into view.

# Two

'WHAT'S happening?' asked James.

'You're not well,' his sister said to the boy on the bed.

'No.' Peter shook his head, trying to clear his thoughts. 'Have you really been waiting?'

'I think so. I didn't know I had until I saw you.'

The ball of light jangled around her head. Then it grabbed at her hair and pulled hard.

'Stop it,' Peter ordered.

'I don't mind. She always does that, doesn't she?'

'Does she? I can't remember.'

James was staring at the bundle of light. It had stopped darting about, anchored for the moment by his sister's hair. Now that it was still he could almost make out a shape in the middle. It was a girl of some sort. Older than his sister, but so tiny, and wearing a lot of make-up that gave her a look that was what he thought people meant when they said someone was 'a bit tarty'. She was well-developed and made him feel uncomfortable the way her body swelled under the same sort of leotard as Peter's. She had four earrings in her left ear, one dangling, one a proper ring and two studs, and she had a stud in her nostril. When she saw that he was staring at her she pushed her tongue out at him, dropped the lock of hair and clattered off into a corner where she hovered discordantly.

'What is it?' James asked.

'It's Tinker Bell,' his sister told him. The bundle broke free from its corner, zoomed across the room in a rage, smacked her face and darted back.

'No,' Peter said. 'Not Tinker Bell. That can't be right.'

'Surely?'

'No. Dead. All dead. That one's called something else. I can't remember.' Peter's face looked more drawn and tired than before. James watched his shadow flickering and darting towards the window. The more tired Peter was the more active the shadow became.

'Something's wrong,' James said. 'I don't understand it. Who are these people?'

'This is Peter,' explained his sister, putting her arm around the boy.

'Peter who?' James looked down at them together on the bed.

'Pain,' said the boy, clutching his body tightly. 'Pain.'

'Pan,' his sister said.

'Peter Pain?' asked James.

'Pain. Help me, Wendy.'

'How does he know who you are?'

'Please. Pain.'

'He knows all of us. Didn't he know you?'

James remembered Peter's odd question, 'Which one are you?' 'Yes,' he said. 'He knew us.'

'Put him to bed. He's ill.'

James and Wendy swivelled Peter around until his head rested on the pillow. Then they pulled the duvet over him. James's hand rubbed against his leotard as he lifted him. It wasn't a smooth material with a spider-web pattern after all; it was made of skeleton leaves stitched together. He remembered that the girl in the bundle of light wore the same.

'What about that?' he said, pointing to the corner.

'She's all right. She's worried about Peter, aren't you?'

A noisy jangling seemed to agree.

'We'll look after him. Don't worry. You *look* like Tinker Bell. Is your name something like hers? Shall I call you Tink?' The bundle made another noise, not unpleasant. 'All right then, Tink. James doesn't believe it yet, but I know you're a fairy.'

James made a noise at the back of his throat to show that he didn't believe it; it would have come out sounding like a mocking laugh if it hadn't been so unpleasant.

'See,' Wendy said. 'He'll take a lot of convincing, but I expect he'll have to come round to it in the end. Come on, James. Sleep in the chair in my room.'

Tink bounced up and down against the ceiling in the corner, jangling most distressingly.

'Don't worry. It's holidays. There's no school tomorrow. Come and wake us up when you hear people moving and we'll keep him under cover. They won't find him.'

Wendy and James crossed the landing. Tink hung two inches above Peter's head, watching him. The wind blew the curtains, casting moonlight on the boy's sick face. A car drove carefully past the house, then all was silent. Slowly, a dark shape slipped out from under the duvet. Peter's shadow, stitched to the soles of his feet, was struggling to get out into the night sky, tugging at the boy to follow him. Peter gave a low moan and turned over in the bed.

Matthew was the first one up in the morning. Tink was tugging Wendy's hair. 'All right. All right.' Her head was fuzzy. She had been dreaming that a strange boy had appeared in James's room in the night. She opened her eyes and saw James sprawled in her chair, a blanket wrapped around his shoulders, his mouth open in sleep and his head tilted oddly to one side. He'll have a stiff neck, she thought. Her hair was caught in something that was tugging at it, and there was a low jangling near her ear. It was very puzzling. Why was James in her room?

It came back to her all in a rush. She sat up quickly, flicking her head off the pillow, and caught a glimpse of the fairy being thrown across the room. This was stupid. It wasn't happening. She ducked quickly as Tink soared back towards her ready to smack her in the face again.

'Sorry, Tink,' Wendy whispered. 'It was an accident.'

The fairy hovered sullenly by James. Wendy could hear a buzzing and roaring noise coming from Matthew's room, interrupted from time to time by bleeps and screams and sirens. Tink looked towards the noise anxiously.

'It's only a game,' Wendy explained. 'On his computer. Things chase each other and get blown up or something.' Tink shrugged and tried to look unconcerned. Then she buzzed at the door like a bluebottle against a window. Wendy scrambled out of bed and followed her.

Peter was still asleep, his head burrowed deep into the pillow, hair twisting out around his face like a halo of bright snakes. He looked tired still, but better. Tink jangled.

'Yes,' said Wendy, who seemed to understand her. 'I'll wake him and warn him it's morning. But it should be all right.'

Wendy shook Peter's shoulder gently. He sprang out of bed, wide awake at once, his hand drawing the dagger from his belt. Tink danced in front of his face, clanging. He brushed her aside.

'Wendy. There you are,' he said to Tink. 'I told you she'd be here.' He threw back his head and crowed. Wendy grabbed at his mouth, stifling him.

'Shsshh. You'll bring Mum and Dad in.'

Peter staggered under her attack. He was a couple of inches smaller than Wendy and he was still weak from his illness. He sat on the bed.

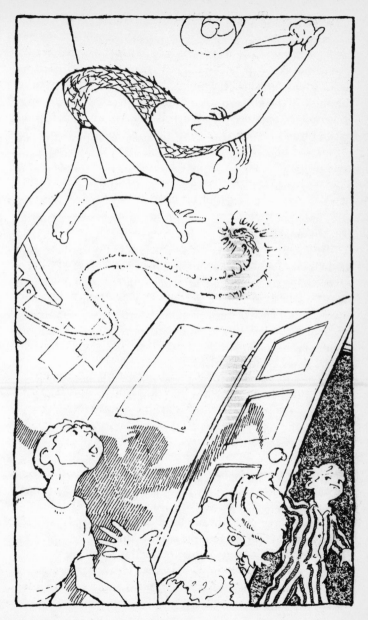

'What's going on?' James asked from the doorway.

'Shut the door and come in. Peter's better.'

'I didn't believe it. I thought it was a dream.'

'Dream,' said Peter contemptuously. 'They always say it's a dream. They always want to come with me, all of them, and then they say afterwards it was a dream. But they know really.' He was sitting on the bed when he started, but as he grew excited he rose up until at the end he was calling down to them from the ceiling and Tink was soaring in circles round him, jangling and clanging and laughing. 'They forget. They all forget or pretend. Come on. It's your turn. Let's go.'

Wendy and James were staring open-mouthed at his performance and didn't see Matthew come in.

'I'm hungry,' he said. 'What's he doing up there? You're all making a lot of noise.' He pointed at Tink. 'That's a funny thing. I've scored seventeen thousand points and nearly killed him but he got away. Who is he?' he asked again, pointing at Peter this time. Matthew was seven and he thought about lots of things at once and spoke about them all at the same time.

'It's Peter,' said Wendy.

'That's right,' Matthew answered. 'I thought he was. Hello, Peter.' Matthew jumped up and down, trying to fly up to the ceiling to him, but of course he couldn't so he began to cry. He was too old to cry at little things like that really, but he was the youngest so he'd never seen how awful it was.

'Shut up,' said Peter. 'You're too little. We don't need you. We need Wendy, and I suppose,' he looked at James, 'I suppose we could do something with you.'

Matthew was making a terrible noise, and fat tears were running down his cheeks. Wendy grabbed a tissue from the box on the floor and pulled a face when she felt how damp it was. She tore out a lot more, wiped her hand and then cleaned Matthew's face.

'Tell him he can come,' she ordered Peter, 'or he'll go

on doing this until Mum comes up and then we're all done for.'

'All right,' Peter said. 'Make him shut up.'

'Can I?' said Matthew. He had stopped crying instantly. 'Can I really?'

'Yes.'

'Go where?' asked James.

'The usual place. But not until it's dark,' said Wendy. 'We can't go yet. Slip back into bed, Peter. You're getting better but you're not well yet. We'll get you some breakfast.'

'It'll be all right,' said James. 'No one comes in here much.' He looked for Peter's shadow, but although the sun was bright in the room he couldn't see it at all.

The children's parents were in the kitchen eating breakfast. Mr Hacker was in shirt sleeves and braces. They were splendid red braces with gold adjusters. His shirt was in bold stripes and he had on a rather dull tie. He ignored the children and went on reading his newspaper. Mrs Hacker pushed some bowls across the table and a jar of rather ferocious muesli.

'I want corn flakes,' said Matthew.

'Corn flakes aren't food,' said his mother. Mr Hacker pretended he was on his own with his newspaper.

'Jack has corn flakes.'

'Then Jack won't grow up properly,' she said.

'I had corn flakes when I stayed with Jack.'

'Then he'll have muesli if he comes to stay with you.'

James and Wendy had nearly finished theirs.

'I bet Peter can have corn flakes whenever he likes. When we go off with Peter I'll have corn flakes every day.'

Wendy and James were horrified and didn't know how to shut Matthew up. Mrs Hacker had a puzzled look on her face. 'Who's Pet– ?'

'Look, old son,' said Mr Hacker. 'You can eat corn flakes until they distend your stomach like an airship when you leave home, but while you're here you eat what you're given. Understand?' And having helped his wife with bringing up the children he folded his newspaper, kissed Mrs Hacker, Wendy, James and Matthew on the tops of their heads and went out to sit by a computer and a telephone in the City all day and make lots of money.

Matthew opened his mouth wide at exactly the moment the door shut and he began to scream. This was Matthew's answer to all problems in his life and twice before breakfast was not at all unusual. Everybody else hated it. Sometimes Mrs Hacker hated it so much that she gave him what he wanted straight away and he shut up. She hardly ever smacked him, because if she did he screamed louder and threw his legs about and that was even worse for her. If she ignored him he carried on screaming until he felt better and forgot what was the matter.

'Can I make him some toast to have in his bedroom?' asked Wendy. 'He'll like that. Would you like that, Matthew?' Matthew nodded. The thought of a silent Matthew munching toast in his bedroom made Mrs Hacker smile again. Wendy made six pieces of toast and smeared them with a healthy sort of margarine and pure fruit spread. She piled them on a plate and poured a huge bowl of muesli and took that as well. 'Just in case,' she said.

James was the first out and he was bounding up the stairs while Wendy stacked the toast.

'All right, dear. Bring the things down and wash them up when you've finished, will you?'

'Yes,' Wendy shouted over her shoulder.

Mrs Hacker gave Matthew a hug, glad that he had stopped that dreadful noise. 'Such a baby,' she whispered to him, wishing that he really was, which was why he still behaved like one, of course. He struggled free and followed the others.

'Matthew,' she called out after him. 'Peter who? We don't know a Peter, do we?'

'Yes,' he called down.

'Where does he live?'

'Second to the right and then straight on till morning.' Then he was gone.

# Three

NOT completely gone. There were things to do first. Peter spat a whole mouthful of muesli out on to the floor.

'What's that?'

'Muesli.'

'It's horrible,' Matthew explained, rather unnecessarily.

Peter poked his finger round in the bowl and pulled out all the raisins and whole nuts and stuffed them into his mouth. 'These are all right,' he said, spraying bits of oat out of his mouth. 'But the rest is muck.'

'Yes,' said Matthew.

James was fussing around with the tissues, cleaning up the muesli Peter had spat on to the floor. His bedroom was always the tidiest in the house. James hated mess. Wendy pushed the toast at Peter and watched him eat it.

'I like white bread better,' he said, but he ate all six slices. Matthew was delighted. 'Jack has white bread. And real butter,' he said.

As soon as Peter had finished eating he sprang up.

'Let's go.'

'Where?' asked James.

'The Neverland. The Neverland, of course,' Matthew yelled.

'We can't,' said Wendy.

'We must,' Peter argued.

'We must. We must,' Matthew chanted.

Peter leaped up and flew into the air, arms out-stretched. Wendy was fearful he would crow again, and he looked as though he might, but stopped himself just in time.

'We must go. Neverland is in trouble.'

James was disturbed to see that a small shadow fol-lowed Peter, much tinier than the one cast in the moon-light, and it didn't move quite in time with him, as if reluctant to follow.

'Not until it's dark,' said Wendy.

'Why not?'

'Because it's the only way to get there. Second to the right and straight on till morning. If we go in the morning we'll never find the way.'

Peter slowly floated down from the ceiling. 'She's right,' he said, landing on the cupboard. 'We'll have to go to-night.'

James wasn't sure. 'I don't know. We ought to tell Mum and Dad.' Matthew looked as though he was going to cry.

There was a small noise outside the door and suddenly it opened and their mother walked in. The children turned their heads to look at her and wondered whatever she was going to say about Peter.

'Half an hour, please,' said their mother. 'Washed. Teeth cleaned. Clothes on.'

'Why?'

'New shoes for school. You go back next week. Half an hour, please.' She shut the door behind her.

'That was close,' said Peter, crawling out from under the bed. He was pale again and one hand went to his side where the pain had been. He rubbed it thoughtfully and screwed his face up as though a pang had run through him.

'Peter?' said Wendy.

'It's all right.'

'We could have said you were new around here and had come in to play and get to know us,' said James.

'She'd remember me,' said Peter. 'If she saw me she'd remember.'

'You mean you know Mum?'

'Of course. I always come back.'

Wendy shook her head. 'Not to Mum. I don't think so.'

'Yes. She sounded the same.'

'How long is it since you last came back?' James asked him.

'I don't know. A long time. But I always come back.' Peter was tired again and the strain of trying to remember was hurting him. 'I don't know.'

'Go back to bed,' said Wendy. 'We'll see you when we get back. You can tell us what's wrong in the Neverland.'

'Neverland,' shouted Matthew. 'We're going to Neverland.'

'I don't know,' said James. 'What if it's dangerous? I don't think we should.'

'Twenty minutes,' shouted a voice up the stairs. 'I want you down here in twenty minutes.' They scrambled round and were hardly much more than ten minutes late, so they only had to wait downstairs another quarter of an hour while their mother checked the timer on the oven for lunch, combed her hair, arranged her credit cards in the leather wallet she carried them in, and did fourteen other things that grown-ups always forget to leave time for when they ask you to be ready to go in half an hour.

It was terrible. The sun blazed down and the streets were hot and dirty. Matthew didn't want the shoes his mother chose for him and he had a crying-temper in the shop, in front of everybody. Other mothers looked accusingly at Mrs Hacker, who was so upset by it that she refused to buy James and Wendy the perfectly sensible shoes they wanted, just so that she could feel better about being a grown-up. James and Wendy didn't have tantrums, they were too old for that, but they sulked. James wore his new shoes home, even though he didn't like them, just because he knew his mother didn't want him to in case he scuffed them and spoiled them. He slyly dragged them along the edges of doorsteps so they were spoiled by the time they got home.

'Oh, just look,' said his mother. 'I don't know why I bother.'

'Nor do I,' Wendy agreed, but not loudly enough for her mother to hear.

James's feet were hot and hurt from the new shoes and when he took them off he found a blister on his right heel. He looked around the room and when he saw that his mother wasn't in there he threw the hated shoes against the wall and swore. It was a very bad word and Matthew was rather impressed. The shoes made a mark on the new wallpaper that had cost Mrs Hacker a lot of money.

'Do they wear shoes in the Neverland?'

'Not if you don't want to,' said Wendy.

'We're going tonight.'

They were late home, so they had to eat lunch before they could go up and see how Peter was. Matthew nearly talked about him again, but Mrs Hacker was so tired after the shopping that all three children could have lined up in front of her and said, 'We're going to fly to Neverland tonight after you've gone to bed, and you may never see us again,' and she would have said, 'That's nice, dears,' and not have heard a word.

As it was, they were so frightened that they might talk about Peter that they hardly said anything at all, and Mrs Hacker grew better-tempered and thought that perhaps they weren't such horrid children after all.

'I think I'll get on with some things in the garden,' she said when they had done the washing-up. That meant that she would prod about with a hoe for five minutes annoying some weeds and then lie down and sleep until teatime.

'I'm going to my room,' said Matthew.

'So am I.'

'Me too.'

Peter was asleep.

'He's always asleep,' said Matthew. 'Like a grown-up.'

'He has been very ill,' said Wendy. 'But I think he's getting better.'

Tink was quiet too. She wasn't ill, but she only really did anything when she was angry or anxious. Wendy had brought Peter a sandwich from the kitchen but he didn't want it. He prowled around James's room, impatient to be away.

'What's this?' he asked.

'It's a dragon.' It was a plastic model James had made from a kit. 'It goes with these.' James opened the cupboard and dragged out an army of elves and an army of trolls. The elves were tall and slim and carried bows and slender swords. The trolls were stumpy, with warty faces and big mouths that hung in wicked slack grins. They were armed with curved daggers and savage double-headed axes. Peter kicked the trolls across the floor.

'Hey,' said James. 'Leave them alone.'

'Trolls stink,' Peter said.

'They always lose,' said James. 'I always make the elves win, but the trolls don't stink, they're good fighters.'

Matthew was delighted. He jumped over the bed and ran around the room. 'Trolls stink! Trolls stink!'

'Trolls stink,' said Peter again, holding his nose.

James wanted to argue but Wendy interrupted. 'Don't worry,' she said. 'It's pirates we need to learn to fight.'

Peter was looking round the room again. 'Pirates?' he asked.

'Yes. You've come to us to help you sort out the trouble in the Neverland. Like you always do.'

But Peter wasn't listening any more. 'There used to be

three beds in here,' he said. 'And the others were younger than you.'

'You were younger too,' Wendy said.

'Was I? I don't remember.'

'You had all your first teeth. Now they're gone.'

Peter bared his teeth. They were sharp, shining and all second ones.

'I thought you didn't grow up,' said James.

'I don't. I can't. I won't.'

'You have,' said Matthew.

'How old are you?'

'All ages. No ages. It's all the same when you never grow up.'

'You're the same age as me,' said James. 'Look.' And he stood next to Peter and sure enough they looked the same age. 'I'm eleven. So you must be eleven too.'

'Perhaps you grow up when you're away from the Neverland,' Wendy suggested. 'So it takes a long time, but the more often you come back the older you get.'

'That would mean that one day you'd be here and you'd grow up completely,' said James. 'Then you wouldn't be able to go back ever.'

Peter shook his head violently.

'That's what happened to the others,' Wendy agreed.

'Others?'

'You remember. Tootles. And Nibs. And Slightly and Curly and the Twins.'

Peter shook his head again. 'No. No, I don't know who they are.'

'Perhaps Neverland itself is getting older,' suggested James, who had been thinking about it. 'So you get older with it.'

'I don't know.'

Tink didn't like all this talk about growing up so she jangled about in front of the children, annoying them.

'No she isn't,' said Peter. 'She'll be all right.'

'What's that?' asked Wendy.

Peter shook his head, but Tink jangled even louder.

'What did she say?'

'She says you're too old already. She says you're grown up.'

They all looked at Wendy. She was thirteen and she was easily the tallest of them. She wasn't as womanly as Tink, but she didn't look much like a girl any more.

'I'm growing up a lot outside,' Wendy said. 'But I haven't inside. Not yet.'

'They go together,' said Peter. 'Perhaps Tink's right. Do you want to be grown up?'

Wendy looked as though she was going to cry.

'Yes,' she said at last. 'I do. But not yet. Really not yet.'

Matthew was bored with all this talk. 'What's it like?' he asked. 'Tell us about the Neverland.'

'What's Hook like?' asked James.

'Hook?'

'Captain Hook.'

'He's dead,' Wendy said. 'The crocodile ate him.'

'Who's Captain Hook?' asked Peter.

The children all fell silent.

'He's your enemy,' said Matthew.

'No, he's dead,' repeated Wendy.

'There aren't any enemies now, are there?' said James hopefully. 'Now that Hook's gone.'

'Oh yes,' said Peter. 'There are still enemies. There are always enemies in the Neverland.'

'But you always beat them,' shouted Matthew. 'You're too quick for them, aren't you? You always win.'

'Yes,' shouted Peter. 'I'm too good for them. I'm too quick. I stab them with my dagger. I . . .' He was floating up again.

Tink jangled at Wendy.

'What is it?' asked Wendy.

Peter sank back down. 'We're losing. We aren't well.'

'Are there still others? Are there Lost Boys?'

'Yes,' said Peter. 'But we need more help. That's why I came.'

'How can we help?'

Peter shrugged his shoulders. 'I don't know. I always come here to get help.'

'But if it isn't Hook,' said James, 'who is the enemy now?'

Peter took a deep breath and rubbed his side where the pain was. 'The Driller.'

He said it in such a dreadful voice that Wendy and James swallowed hard and looked worried. Matthew jumped up and down. 'The Driller,' he yelled. 'I can beat him. I can beat the Driller. I know how to.'

'You,' said Peter. 'You're too small. You can't beat the Driller.'

'Well, I nearly can. I nearly did this morning while you were still asleep. I got seventeen thousand points before he drilled me. I'll beat him soon.'

'You're stupid,' said Peter. 'You're only a baby. You don't know what you're talking about.'

Matthew's cheeks went very red and he opened his mouth to scream, but Wendy spoke first.

'Show him, Matthew. Prove to him you're not a stupid baby. Show him the Driller.'

'Come on,' shouted Matthew. 'This way. Into my room.'

Peter hung back. 'He's here? He's really here?'

'Yes.'

'He followed me from the Neverland. You know him. It's a trap.' Peter flew up to the ceiling and drew out his knife. His shadow flickered out to twice his height, drawing him to the open door and to Matthew's bedroom. Tink jangled around his head.

'He was here first,' said Matthew. 'Before you came. I've been playing him for weeks now. I had him for my birthday. Come and see. I've nearly learned how to beat him.'

Peter made a brave face, as though he were being

forced to walk the gangplank, and followed Matthew. Tink clattered and clanged nervously. The shadow led the way eagerly and was the first to leap into Matthew's bedroom. It was a small room, right at the top of the big old house. It had been intended for a servant to sleep in, and with Matthew's bed, his wardrobe, cupboard and desk there was no room for even a child to hide. And it was empty. Peter's face relaxed its look of grim courage. Tink quietened down and hovered, more or less still. The shadow came to a disappointed rest.

'He's not here,' said Peter. 'I knew it.'

Matthew pushed the on/off switch of his computer and the screen began to glow greenly. Peter tensed when the bleeps signalled that it was ready to take the software. Matthew slid the game disk into its slot and tapped the keyboard. An image of trees and a curving coastline drew itself on the screen.

Peter hissed. 'Pirate's Cove.'

Boulders led up from the beach to the entrance of a maze of tunnels. In the distance a lake's edge rippled brightly.

'He's behind a boulder,' James warned.

Peter stood, a horrified look on his face.

'He often starts behind a rock,' said Matthew. 'I can normally escape from him then, but if he gets into the tunnels or over the lake into the desert I've lost.'

Peter's shadow had lengthened across the room and played over the computer screen.

'I didn't know there was a desert,' said James.

'The Great Sand Wastes,' said Peter.

'I only found it this morning,' said Matthew. 'Funny, I've been playing him for weeks now and I thought I knew all the program, but this morning, just when I thought I'd beaten him in a boat on the lake, he got to the other side and we were in a desert.'

'Wow.'

'Yeah. I was lost and he jumped out from behind a sand

dune and drilled me.'

There was a wet, splatting noise behind them. Peter's face was green and he was shivering. He had been sick.

'It must have been the toast,' said Wendy. 'I'll see to it. You get into my bed and have another lie-down.' She took him to her room and came back a few minutes later with a bowl of hot water and disinfectant and a floor cloth. Matthew was chasing the Driller into the cave entrance to the tunnel system.

'What does he look like?' she asked.

'Horrid,' said Matthew. 'Really yucky.'

'You can't really say,' said James. 'He's only a bit of a shape on the screen. I think he must be a robot with a big drill in his hand.'

'No,' said Matthew. 'He's a sort of man, but like a monster. Not a robot anyway. He's got blood, but it's purply blue. And the drill isn't . . .'

'Oh, you're making it up,' said James. 'You can't see.'

'Yes I can.' Matthew was in danger of crying. 'He's got very ginger hair and a scar on his face and a hooked nose and a moustache.' His face was getting redder.

'All right,' said James. 'Red hair and a scar. If you say so.'

Matthew was pushing the 'fire' button on the keyboard all the time, paying no attention to where his shots went. Suddenly, the Driller jumped out of a side tunnel that he had left unguarded and there was a loud buzzing noise and the whole screen flashed stars and it was over.

'Got you,' said James.

'I never escape him in those tunnels,' said Matthew. 'They're the worst.'

The Neverland was drawing closer.

# *Four*

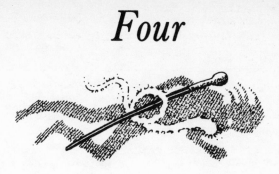

Peter felt a little better after being sick. He sat on Wendy's bed chewing the sandwich.

'I wish we could go,' Matthew complained.

'It will soon be bedtime,' Wendy encouraged him.

But it wasn't. Mrs Hacker woke up in the garden feeling rather light-headed and dizzy and was annoyed and ashamed of how little work she had done, so she gathered the children together and set them to work to pull up weeds, spray the roses, scrape out the grass that grew between the cracks in the crazy paving, brush out the charcoal ash in the barbeque, trim the hedge and tidy up the tools in the shed.

'I've done my bit,' she announced, 'I'll make some tea while you get on.'

Then, after tea, which was late because the shopping had made the whole day late, it was time for Matthew to have his bath and get ready for bed.

'Your father will be home late tonight,' she said anxiously. 'So you'll have to go without seeing him.' Matthew always used this as an excuse to stay up late and Mrs Hacker couldn't bear the thought of another tantrum.

'That's all right,' said Matthew, and he ran up the stairs two at a time, pulling off his clothes ready for the bath. He was back down in no time, hair wet and wearing his pyjamas.

'Good night.'

'Darling,' said his mother. 'Are you all right?'

'Oh yes. Very tired.' Matthew proved how tired he was by giving a horribly wide yawn without putting his hand over his mouth. His mother winced.

James could hear the bleeps and screeches from the Driller program when he went for his bath. James didn't wear pyjamas, he slept in a pair of boxer shorts, so he pulled his dressing gown on to go down and say good night.

'I'll come up when your father's home,' said his mother.

'All right. Shall I run your bath?'

'Yes, please,' said Wendy.

'Come on,' James ordered Peter.

'Where?' Peter had been asleep again in Wendy's bed.

'To my room. Wendy's coming up.'

'I'll wait.'

'She's having a bath and getting ready for bed.'

'So?'

Tink jangled. James looked up in surprise. She had been lying in a pile of clothes in an open drawer and he hadn't seen her there. It was her angry noise.

'Oh, all right,' agreed Peter, 'but I don't see why.'

James turned to go out.

'What are you wearing?' Peter asked. He stretched out his hand as though afraid to touch James.

'My dressing gown.'

It was the one he'd had for Christmas and he had forgotten how excited he had been when he first saw the dark-blue material with the stars on the front. It tied with a red belt. The sleeves were wide and fell dramatically away from the wrists. If James tried to wear it for breakfast he knocked things over on the table and dragged the cuffs through the margarine. On the back were pictures of the moon and a dragon and a unicorn and a lightning bolt. His father had bought it for him because he thought it would go with the elves and the troll army. 'There's a stick that goes with it,' explained James. 'Come and see.'

When Peter saw James seize the stick he drew in his breath sharply. James turned around to let Peter see him from all sides.

'Don't know what this is for,' he said, waving the stick.

A bell jangled.

'Stupid,' sang Tink.

'What's that?' James asked.

'Nothing,' Peter said.

'We don't need him,' Tink jangled. 'Just steal the wizard's cloak from him and the magic wand. We'll do it ourselves.'

'No,' murmured Peter. 'I think it has to be him.'

Wendy pulled on a kaftan over her light summer nightdress when she went downstairs to say goodnight. It was too hot for it really but she thought, I'm not flying anywhere just in my nightie. And it may have been her thought, or it may have been the way the kaftan fell sinuously over her, but in the next room Tink shivered and this made her clang.

'Princess,' said Wendy's mother when she bent to kiss her good night. She always called her that when she wore the kaftan. 'You're my eastern princess,' her father had said the first time she wore it.

Wendy was reading in bed when she heard Mrs Hacker go in to Matthew and make him turn off the computer and get into bed. She went to James next. Wendy knew Peter would be hiding and quite safe; but she wondered what he would be thinking of the good-night kisses, and she remembered how another Wendy had let him believe that kisses were called thimbles.

'You'll put your light out soon, won't you?' her mother

said. 'I expect you'll still be awake when your father gets in.'

Wendy waited another ten minutes after her mother had gone down and then she collected Matthew to take him to James's room. Despite the excitement Matthew had gone straight to sleep when his mother closed his door. Wendy had to be careful to wake him gently so he wouldn't call out. At the top of the stairs they could hear music drifting up from below. James was standing ready in his dressing gown when they opened the door. The windows were wide and the rim of the moon was just appearing over the houses opposite. Peter's shadow was clear again. When the children walked in it snaked away from the window and fell for a second over Wendy's face. It stroked down her body, then sprang away, pulling Peter to the window.

'Let's fly,' he ordered them. 'Look.' He soared up. Matthew jumped up and down but James and Wendy stayed still.

'We need the fairy dust,' said Wendy, 'or it won't work.'

Peter was disappointed. He liked to play his trick on the children and watch them helplessly trying to fly before he showed them the secret.

'Oh, all right. Tink. Come here.'

Tink put up a show of resisting but she knew that she would have to in the end, so she let Peter grab hold of her and shake her over James. The very tiniest shower of dust spilled over Matthew as well by mistake and he soared up immediately. James quickly followed. Then Peter shook the dust on Wendy and she leaped up but came straight back down and twisted her ankle. She tried again but couldn't even leave the ground. Peter shook Tink over Wendy until the fairy squealed but it wouldn't work.

'I think you've grown up too much to fly,' said James.

'We'll leave you behind,' said Matthew.

'Please,' Wendy begged. 'Please try again.' But nothing would work.

'We can't go without you,' James said. 'We'll all stay.'

'No!' Peter shouted. 'We've got to go.'

'I'm going,' said Matthew. He swept over to Wendy unsteadily like a sparrow fluttering through leaves. He gave her a quick kiss and headed for the open window. 'Here's Dad,' he yelled. 'Get a move on.' Tink followed him. James hovered in the air, frightened to let Matthew go on his own, but unwilling to leave without Wendy.

'Please,' he said to Peter.

'Thimbles,' Peter shouted. 'Thimbles and goodbye.' Then he too sped across the room to kiss Wendy. As his lips met hers for a quick kiss the shadow darted between their faces, blotting out the moon, and when their lips joined in a shy, long kiss Wendy's feet left the floor and she rose up with Peter, so that when the kiss was over she hung uncertainly, but quite clearly flying on her own. Her face was disturbed and Peter looked as if the pain was about to send him plummeting down again when suddenly he grinned, threw his head back and crowed. The shadow dragged him towards Matthew, who was about to leave through the open window.

'We're off,' Matthew shouted.

'Your wand,' Peter yelled. He span round the room, seized the stick that went with James's dressing gown and flung it to him.

James caught it. 'My what?'

But Peter was gone, and Matthew, and Wendy was urging him on, 'Come on, James. Come on.'

Below, on the pavement, Mr Hacker heard Peter's whoop of triumph. He looked up just in time to see one, two, three, *four* people flying round and round in James's bedroom, with a bundle of light darting round them. He ran at full speed into the house, shouting to his wife, taking the stairs three at a time as he ran up. When he flung open the bedroom door the curtain at the open window rose up and the moonlight fell on his lost and bewildered face.

The moon rode up over the rooftops like a pirate galleon on a calm sea. Peter soared ahead of the others, his slim body a shadow sharply picked out against the bright background of the sky. Tink, faster than the eye could follow, danced round and round him in delight. James's face was grim and determined as he came behind Peter; his dressing gown flowed out behind him and he pointed the long stick ahead as though it were pulling him along. He kept his eyes up and ahead as much as he could; if he looked down his head went fuzzy and he began to lose height.

'This is it,' shouted Peter. 'Second to the right.' He made a sharp banking turn.

'And straight on till morning,' Matthew joined in. He didn't care where he looked. He loved flying. He didn't bother to lie flat out with arms outstretched like James, but bounced and tumbled up and down, turning somersaults through the air until, at last, when he nearly tied himself up in some electric cables, Wendy dipped down and took his hand and led him quietly beside her until he could get used to flying and be more sensible.

I'm glad I put my kaftan on, she thought, but a part of her wished that she could be in her nightdress, the thin material flowing gracefully behind her, the breeze caressing her bare arms. When this picture came into her mind she took a sickening dip and started to drop to earth. 'I'm glad I'm in this kaftan,' she said out loud and rescued herself from her fall.

'Wheeee,' Matthew yelled. 'Let's all fall.'

Wendy gripped his hand tighter and led him through the night.

'How?' asked Mr Hacker. 'I don't understand. How could it happen?'

Mrs Hacker stroked her temples where they were beginning to throb with grief. 'It's Peter,' she said helplessly. 'He's come back.'

'Peter?' Mr Hacker was very frightened for his children

so he tried to make himself feel better by being angry with his wife. 'What do you mean? Peter?'

'It's so awful,' she said. Her head was impossibly painful and she sat in exactly the place on the bed where James had first seen Peter. 'Such a lot of . . .'

'Peter who?' demanded her husband, ignoring what she was saying. 'Peter?'

'. . . pain,' Mrs Hacker finished.

'Peter Pain?'

'Did I say that?' she asked. 'I don't think so. I don't remember.'

Wendy had lost sight of Peter. The moon had sunk below the horizon and they were flying by starlight.

'Where are you? Peter?'

'Pain,' said a voice beside her. Peter had dropped back from the lead and was flying alongside, rubbing where the pain was.

'Let's rest.'

'James.'

James lowered his staff and turned like a swimmer in the water. They stopped in a circle and hung there, treading air.

'Peter's not well,' Wendy explained.

'And there's still a long way to go,' he added.

'So we need to rest.'

Peter showed them how to fly above the clouds and lower themselves slowly so they could rest on them. He's much nicer than he used to be, thought Wendy. Because he's not well he doesn't bother to play so many tricks on people. She was pleased to see that Peter was even helping Matthew, who was having trouble judging the distance, so he could make a soft landing. In the old days, she thought, he'd let Matthew hurt himself and then he'd just laugh and show off.

Soon they were all, except Tink, who didn't need a rest, sitting or lying on high clouds drifting towards morning and the Neverland.

In the dark, at the mouth of the cave entrance to the tunnel system, a man suddenly looked up into the stars and smiled a cruel smile. He was tall with a hooked nose and a scar on his cheek. His hair and moustache were fiery red. His right arm hung heavy at his side; he lifted it, pointing towards the darkest part of the sky, and instead of ending in a hand there was a powerful drill. As his smile broadened to show teeth made of sharpened steel, the drill buzzed at his wrist, slowly at first, but then increasing to a whining speed that echoed into the cave.

'What's up?' asked a hoarse voice from inside.

'See.'

A low figure, only half the height of the Driller, stumbled on broad feet into the starlight. Its legs were thick and bandy. Everything about it was thick: its nose, its fingers, its coarse brown hair, its neck, and especially the wooden handle of the cruel double-headed axe it carried. It squinted up, following the direction of the drill.

'Can't see.'

'He's coming, Jooks,' said the Driller. 'And he's bringing the others with him.'

The troll pushed his ugly broad head back into the cave.

'He's coming, boys. Come and see.'

There was a shuffling of big feet and other trolls came out. They crinkled up their faces in the fresh air, which smelled as rancid to them as the foul air of their caves would smell to ordinary people, and they screwed up their eyes against the stars, which were painfully bright. Light hurts trolls and they can see best when the darkness is complete. First came Strakey, then Slee, then Skylights, who tripped on a stone in the mouth of the cave and knocked into the Driller.

'Filthy troll,' he snarled as the smelly body smeared greasily against his impeccable shirt with broad stripes.

'Sorry,' Skylights began to apologise fearfully, but the drill shot towards him whining with speed and bored straight into his head between his eyes. The troll dropped to the floor, dead instantly.

'Cheko, Loder. To the pit,' shouted the Driller.

Two more trolls shuffled out into the night air and stooped to pick up the body of Skylights. Cheko took hold of his arms and Loder picked up his legs to drag him back in. Loder was especially careful for he didn't want to trip against the Driller, and picking Skylights up was quite difficult because Loder's hands were fixed on to his wrists backwards. When the other trolls walked in their peculiar bent-backed, bandy-legged way their knuckles dragged on the ground. Loder's palms dragged if he didn't keep his arms higher than the others. With many grunting complaints about how heavy he was they dragged his body to one of the many shafts in the tunnels that fell deep into the burning heart of the ground below the Neverland. Skylight's body bounced against the sides of the deep shaft. Minutes later, a nasty smell of greasy burning drifted up.

'I hope there isn't any danger there,' said Mr Hacker. 'Is there?'

'Well, there's always danger in the Neverland,' said his wife. 'Pirates and the crocodile and things. There were red Indians but I don't remember whether they were friends or enemies.'

Mr Hacker snorted. This is a most unpleasant thing to do and much nastier to hear than to read about.

'Games,' he said. 'I'm worried about them flying off. What if they fall into the sea? What if they crash? And why? Why did they go?'

Mrs Hacker thought she knew why but she didn't want to say so.

'I'll let them know what I think about flying off when I get them back.' Mr Hacker was walking up and down the room and now he pointed out into the night sky.

'George,' said his wife. She stood up and put her hand into his. 'Don't you understand? They might not come back.'

Mr Hacker lowered his pointing finger and plunged his hand into his pocket. He remembered that he wasn't really angry at all, that he had been pretending. He remembered that he was frightened for his children and frightened for his wife and frightened for himself.

'What, never?'

She shook her head. 'Never.'

Hand in hand they stared hopelessly through the open window.

# Five

DAWN was breaking in the Neverland. The Driller prowled away into the jungly undergrowth where he conducted a never-ending search for the people he hated most. The jungle was hot and sticky, muddy underfoot, with stinging plants that lashed his flesh as he passed. He hated it. He had never so much as heard the rustle of a Lost Boy in all his searches. Turning towards the beach he decided it was time to try another plan.

The light grew brighter. The trolls shuffled back into their stinking cave to find dirty corners to sleep in while the hateful sun warmed the stretch of white sand that curved round the blue sea of the bay.

Peter, James, Wendy and Matthew stirred from sleep on the clouds as the sun dusted their faces with pink and gold.

In a part of the jungle far from the questing Driller there was a ratlike shuffling that came from under a mossy bank dotted with woodbine, wild thyme, eglantine and oxlips, violets and musk roses; for the scenery changes very suddenly in the Neverland. The woodbine was pushed aside and a sore, red face stared out. It coughed, screwed up its small eyes against the early sun, breathed deeply, coughed again and then spat. After that it looked a little more comfortable. Shoulders followed the face, then a waist and legs and finally feet. Other boys followed: two dirty identical twins who held hands and seemed to be joined together at the palms; a boy so thin that he looked as though he would snap like a dry twig if anyone tried to cuddle him; then a fat boy with a piggy nose and a pair of piggy eyes behind a pair of broken spectacles, one lens good, the other starred and smashed; last of all came a sly-looking boy who managed to scramble out of the hole without once taking his hands out of his pockets, an exercise so difficult that the speed he needed to get out carried him right to the other side of the clearing, where he wandered nonchalantly whistling as though he didn't recognise the others. The Lost Boys had got up.

Peter stood on the cloud, stretched his arms up and then leaped down into the air. He circled right under the cloud's belly and soared up the other side like a swimmer diving under a great raft.

'The Neverland,' he crowed. 'Look.'

The others scrambled to their feet. Matthew slipped off the edge and went plummeting down. He screamed in terror, then, remembering that he could fly, swooped round, banked against the rising sun and flew back up to the others, screaming half in frustrated temper and fear from his fall and half in unstoppable joy in his flight. Tears and screams of delight mingled in his little face.

Wendy and James let their eyes follow Peter's finger and all four of them stepped off the cloud. They fell into flying formation like four geese strung out in a skein across the sky. Below them the silver-white sand of the beach curved round Pirate's Cove. A line of boulders led up to a cave mouth in the lip of a dense jungle. To the east of the cave a wide lake rippled out, blue and sparkling in the morning sun, and beyond that, undulating gently to a mysterious horizon, stretched the endless shifting tracts of the Great Sand Wastes. It was too much for the eyes or the mind to take in. Matthew thought he saw a shadow slip out from the fringe of the jungle and crouch behind the boulder nearest to the yawning mouth of the cave, but the ground was so far below that he could not be sure.

'What's that?' shouted James.

'I don't know,' Peter answered.

The decomposing body of a galleon lay half beached at the low-water mark, still anchored to the sea bed. It rose up with the tide, floated unsteadily, then sank back as the waters receded. Each raising and lowering dragged a little more at the rotting timbers, breaking new holes in them, snapping more bones of the skeleton of spars and struts that held it together. One day, rotted with its own motion, it would disintegrate completely and for ever and drift out piecemeal into the open sea.

'It's the Jolly Roger,' said Wendy.

Peter ignored them and flew on, but the three children stopped and hovered over it so that Peter was obliged to turn and fly back to them.

'Hook's ship,' said James.

'I don't know. It's always been there, I suppose.'

To the west of the cove the jungle spread right down to the water's edge. It was from here that a splashing drew their attention away from the ship. Something had launched itself from the undergrowth and was swimming towards the wrecked ship. Matthew darted off and swept over it. His movement caught the creature's eye. It stopped, briefly, and raised its head to watch him, opening a long, narrow jaw lined with jagged teeth.

'The crocodile,' said James.

Matthew returned to the others and they watched the reptile swim out to the corpse of the galleon, drift all around it hopefully and then make a disappointed return to the overhanging trees.

'It goes there every day,' Peter explained. 'I don't know why.'

The shape that Matthew had seen flicker between the cave and the boulder took advantage of the children's interest in the galleon. It darted from rock to rock, keeping to the shadows. At last it reached the water's edge. Hard eyes scanned sea and sky from beneath red eyebrows. When Matthew flew near to the crocodile and the brute opened its mouth, a low buzzing started at the end of the Driller's right arm. Whenever he was excited or angry the drill began to twist of its own accord. The greater the feelings the swifter it turned. The Driller only had a mild hope this time that Matthew would fly out of control and be snapped into the crocodile's jaws, so the drill revolved with only a slow interest. His thin lips turned up at the edges under the red moustache as he imagined the wide jaws snapping over the small boy. He was pleased to see Peter again, and especially pleased to see these children.

'Come on, my beauties,' he sang. 'Come to Driller. Come to see my trolls.' The drill buzzed faster.

Colin sat with his back to a tree, knees bent, fumbling through his pockets, looking for a match to light his cigarette.

'Shouldn't have them,' said the fat boy with the spectacles. His name was Bins.

Colin spat on the floor of the jungle and carried on searching through his pockets.

'Give me ass-mar,' the fat boy went on. 'Makes me cough.' As if to prove it he began to splutter with a rattling noise in his chest.

'Go away then,' said Colin, who had found a match and was dragging the smoke down into his lungs. Then he started to cough as well, but he always did when he lit the first cigarette of the day.

'I'm hungry,' said the thin boy.

'So are we,' said the twins, both together. They were still holding hands.

'Get a fish then,' said Colin. 'I'm not bothered.'

'What if he's there?' snapped Bins.

'You can't be hungry,' said Colin. 'You're too fat.'

Bins looked away, screwing up his face so that he wouldn't cry.

'He's always there,' said the twins. 'Always when we're hungry. He waits for us.'

'Buzzzzz,' said the boy with his hands in his pockets. 'Buzzzzz.' And he laughed. The twins, who were the smallest of the Lost Boys, began to cry, both together. Bins shouted at him.

'Shut up, Looter. Just shut up.'

Looter laughed again, but he stopped the buzzing noise.

Then there was a jangling in the air and a disturbance up above the boy's heads. They all looked up except Colin, who took another draw on his cigarette and kept his elbows on his knees and his eyes down to the ground.

'It's Tink,' the twins shouted. 'Peter's back!'

Tink clanged above them. In the Neverland her jangling was real words and the boys could understand everything she said.

'He's on his way,' she said. 'And he's brought them with him. He wants food, and he wants it straight away. He's in a foul temper.'

The twins ran into the hole in the mossy bank. There was a terrific crunching and scraping and they came out looking very unhappy.

'Nothing,' said Looter.

They shook their heads.

'You must get some,' Tink shrieked unpleasantly.

'Count me out,' said Colin.

'I can't go. Not with my ass-mar.' Bins started to wheeze again.

The very thin boy stepped forward.

'We got to eat,' he said. 'Let's get some food.'

'Let Peter get it himself. Let him get some for us,' argued Looter.

'He's ill,' said the thin boy.

'And he's furious,' shouted Tink. 'He'll bring the Driller here, then he'll fly off and leave you to it. He wants fresh food waiting for him, not that rubbish from the bins.'

Bins slithered off into the jungle.

'Watch out! Driller!' Tink screamed.

'Buzzzzz,' called Looter. Then he laughed at the way Bins popped back out of the trees and into the clearing. 'Come on,' he said. 'You and me, Hardly?' The thin boy nodded. 'We'll draw the Driller away from the beach. Then the rest of you get some fish or something.'

'All right,' agreed the twins. Bins moved over to be with them silently. 'Come on, Colin.'

'Not coming,' said Colin.

'You're a pig,' said Bins. 'Just a lazy pig.' His face caught the sun and the good lens of his broken specs flashed angrily. Colin pinched out the end of his cigarette so he wouldn't waste any tobacco, stood up and crossed the clearing menacingly towards Bins. The fat boy backed behind the twins.

'Leave him,' shouted Looter. 'It needs all of you.' Colin nodded. 'We'll get the Driller, OK? You watch him disappear and then you're in business.'

The clearing emptied, leaving Tink alone, laughing.


Mr and Mrs Hacker sat miserably at breakfast. They had pale faces and dark rings under their eyes. They had not slept well. Mr Hacker's newspaper lay unopened next to his plate.

'I wish they were here.'

'You'd only hide behind that paper if they were.' His wife wanted to be kind to him but she couldn't help herself.

'Would I? Yes, I suppose so. I always did.'

'Why aren't you reading it?'

'I don't know. It always seemed so important before. Now I couldn't care what's in it.' He picked it up but only glared at the front page and then let it drop back on to the table.

'I'm sorry,' said his wife. 'Eat up your breakfast.'

He held a spoonful of muesli up to his mouth but then put it back into the bowl.

'You know,' he said. 'This stuff really is awful, isn't it?'

'Shall we buy something else?'

'Some corn flakes?'

'Do you think that would work?'

'I don't know. It's worth a try.'

Before he left for the office Mr Hacker went into the three bedrooms his children had flown away from. He was looking for reasons why they had gone, promises that they would return. By the side of each bed lay a brand-new pair of sensible shoes. He sat down in Matthew's room in front of the computer, flicking the switch on and off, watching the green light glow and fade. Absently he picked up the Driller software and slipped it into his jacket pocket.

'They always come back from there, don't they?' he asked his wife.

'Oh yes. Always.'

But they both knew that wasn't true.

'Goodbye then.'

'Goodbye, George.' His wife kissed him. 'There's no real danger.'

'No.'

'It's beautiful,' said Wendy. 'It's all so beautiful. Just as I imagined it.'

Peter crowed. All trace of his pain and illness had gone. He was proud of the Neverland and he wanted to show off to Wendy and the others. They followed Peter as he rose into the air and soared over the Neverland. Far below them on the beach were their four shadows. Three, the children's, followed them exactly, stroking after them over the sands, but Peter's fought against the sun, trying, and failing, to break away and glide snakelike over the ground and into the jungle or the cave.

They saw the lagoon and the curved shore. They flew so low over the jungle that they were able to reach down and let the tops of the trees brush against their hands. A flock of parrots, gold and blue and green, spread wings more beautiful and elegant than could be imagined and lifted their round heads and hooked beaks over the trees to squawk at the children. Banking away from the jungle, with its dense green mysteries and tiny hidden clearings, the children swooped over the inland lake. The water was so pure and clear that they could see right through to its depths, down to the rocky bed. Swarms of silver fish danced delightedly beneath them. At the other side of the lake a sprinkling of palm trees on the bank were the only flash of green for miles and miles as the yellow mounds of sand ran on for ever.

'Let's turn back,' said Peter.

'No,' Wendy argued. 'This is my desert. Look.' She spread her arms wide and the kaftan opened out like wings, the fine material waving in the hot, dry desert wind.

They flew until Wendy saw plumes of sand lifting from the dunes. A narrow line of camels and people on foot dragged in single file through the Great Sand Wastes. Three magnificent horses pranced alongside the caravan, darting and rearing with riders on their backs.

'Who are they?' she asked.

'Don't know. We never come over here. No one does.'

Wendy was afraid that if they flew too close they would disturb the lonely procession in the desert. She did not see the eyes of one of the riders lift from above a veil and squint questioningly and unbelievingly up.

'I'm hot,' said Matthew.

'And thirsty,' said James.

'And tired,' said Peter. 'It's time to see the Lost Boys.' They wheeled round and set off for the palm trees, the lake and the jungle. Peter rubbed his side thoughtfully and his face was drawn again.

It was silent beneath them when they reached Pirate's Cove again. From the west of the bay, beyond where the waves licked the jungle, a column of smoke rose up and the breeze carried it towards them with a faint echo of metallic clanks and heavy thuds.

'What's over there?' asked James, pointing with his staff.

'We never go there either. We like the jungle and the beach.'

Just at the moment that Wendy had made Peter fly on over the desert, Looter and Hardly had crouched at the jungle's edge looking out for the Driller. Bins, the twins and Colin were hidden at the other side of the cave where they could watch what happened. Already the sun had passed its highest point and was beginning to sink into early afternoon.

There was a pool at the eastern end of the cove. At high water the tide covered it completely, filling it with fish, crabs, prawns and lobsters, so easy to catch when they were trapped at low tide that the Lost Boys never had to worry about food. Except when the Driller was there. Now, he sat at the edge of the pool dangling his bare feet in the water. He held a huge, black lobster in his one hand, its legs flailing, pincers opening and closing helplessly.

'Come on, boys,' he called. 'Lobster for dinner. Drop him in the pot.'

He knew the boys were hungry. He knew they would be watching him now. He tossed the lobster into the air; it span, hung for a second, then fell towards him. The Driller flicked his head to one side and caught the creature in his mouth. The lobster's scaly casing cracked between his steel teeth. Shaking his head like a terrier with a rat the Driller squeezed the life from the lobster. Its legs flickered, then stilled. Its pincers gaped open. The Driller dropped the lobster's body from his mouth, tore the raw flesh from its claws and sucked the empty shells. It flung the rest away.

'Come on, boys,' he sang again. 'Come for a lovely lobster. Drop him in the pot. Plenty more in the pool.'

Hardly and Looter braced themselves. They were in the chief danger now. They stepped out of the trees near the water's edge.

'Come on then,' shouted Looter. 'Bring it over.'

The Driller smiled, his teeth flashing the sun across to the boys. 'Help yourself.' He swept his hand over the surface of the pool. The drill revolved slowly.

'Bring us one.'

'Very well. I'll bring it home to you.'

'Just here. Just to the edge of the beach.'

'Oh no, no, no. Please. Allow me to deliver it, to cook it for you, to serve it with a rich garlic mayonnaise.' The drill was gathering speed but the Driller made no move from the pool. He longed to find the Lost Boys' home.

'All right.'

'Don't,' whispered Hardly.

'It's all right, I won't.'

'What's that?' yelled the Driller. 'What do you say?'

'Come on home with us,' shouted Looter. 'We need the food badly.'

The Driller lunged suddenly into the water and dragged out another lobster. The arm of his striped shirt was drenched.

'Will this do?'

'Yes.'

'For all of you? Come, come. You must need more. Come to the pool and get another to go with it.'

Once by the pool, out on the open beach, the boys would be powerless. The Driller was quicker and stronger. It was only by staying in the jungle that they could escape him, using the tangle of trees and the hidden paths that they knew.

'One's enough. It's for the twins. They're ill. They've got to eat.'

'Ill?'

'Yes.'

'You're all ill. I see you. I see how you hurt. How you throw up.'

'They're worse. They're weak. Can't move. They need food straight away.'

'Come on, then.'

'Bring it to them. You won't hurt them? Not while they're really ill. That wouldn't be fair.'

'No,' agreed the Driller. 'That wouldn't be fair.' The drill speeded up. 'I'll come.'

'Right.' Looter was doing all the talking. Hardly held his breath and kept one hand touching the tree behind him so that he knew he was in safe range of the jungle.

'Meet me halfway?' asked the Driller. 'No danger. I wouldn't hurt you while the dear twins were ill, would I? That wouldn't be fair.'

'All right,' agreed Looter. He stepped out of the shadow of the jungle and into the bright sunlight on the beach.

'Don't,' hissed Hardly, who hadn't moved.

Looter took three paces, then stopped. The Driller sprang up from the pool and bore quickly down on him.

'Come on, then, boy.'

Looter took another two paces. He was still far from the middle of the beach but he looked to Hardly horribly exposed and in danger. The Driller was five paces from him when Looter turned and sped back to the cover of the trees. The Driller stopped. He was so near that the boys could hear the clacking of the lobster's claws and the humming of the drill.

'Oh, dear,' said the Driller. 'And I so much wanted to look after the dear twins, to get them nice and strong for our chases again. We all enjoy the chases so much, don't we?'

Looter and Hardly could see over the Driller's shoulder. The twins and Colin and Bins had broken cover at the other side of the bay and were nearly at the poolside. It was too soon. They would never get back to safety in time if the Driller saw them. They must get him into the jungle.

'Hurry,' said Looter quickly. 'Bring the lobster. This way.'

He turned and made as if to go through the trees.

'No!' rapped the Driller. 'Come out to meet me. You know I hate the jungle. I get lost in there. Come to me or I'll go back to the pool with my lovely lobster.'

Looter had to risk stepping back on to the sand or the Driller would turn and see the others.

'All right,' he said.

Colin had scooped a large parrot fish out of the pool and was holding it triumphantly above his head. It gleamed blue and green and silver in the sun. Bins had just pulled out a huge crab and was already on his way back to the jungle.

That's enough, thought Looter. Don't bother with any more. Get back, quickly. That's enough. But the twins were determined to bring something as well. Still holding hands they leaned over the edge of the pool together grabbing at a huge lobster.

Go, Looter urged them silently. Go!

Something in the boy's face alerted the Driller. At first he thought it was just fear that they were so close and the drill hummed its pleasure at being able to frighten him, but as Looter stood, doing nothing, his suspicions were roused. Noticing the direction of the boy's eyes, the Driller turned his head. He saw Bins disappearing into the undergrowth with his crab, Colin with his huge parrot fish, and the twins trawling the water with their hands. He yelled the same very bad word that James had used and the drill squealed into life. He dropped the lobster and ran to the pool.

Hardly turned and immediately darted into the jungle, but with amazing courage Looter whipped his hands out of his pockets and dashed at the Driller. He tackled him low from behind. The Driller fell awkwardly in the sand. He clutched at Looter and nearly caught his ankle. Looter scrambled away, kicking sand at the Driller, and secured the trees.

Colin was already invisible when the Driller regained his feet. Looter's tackle had given them all time to escape. Or it would have done if the twins had not been terrified when they heard the Driller's yell and the squeal of the drill. They both lunged forward to sprint away, lost their footing on the rocky edge of the pool and fell in. All the fish and crabs and prawns and lobsters fled away. The twins were still trying to clamber out of the pool when the Driller was on top of them. One hand dragged them out and the drill screamed in their faces.

# Six

'HOME,' crowed Peter. He soared over the jungle and dropped suddenly into the flower-filled clearing. The air was cooler there, not filled with the sticky heat of the dark-green trees with their thick succulent leaves. A gentle brook broke through at one side and shivered in a silver snake's trail through the sweet grass. The children all stooped over it, burying their faces in the clear water, sucking it gratefully into their mouths. Peter grabbed large handfuls of it and drenched his hair and the back of his neck. When he lifted his head away from the water his face was lit with a wicked smile, eyes bright with challenge and arrogance. He belonged more to the woods and water than he did to the air he flew through so confidently and gracefully. It was as though he had been made at the same time as the leaves and the flowers and grass and he spoke the same language. The stream had gathered his hair, usually tight to his head, into two branches that stuck out from his forehead like short twisted horns.

Wendy, having drunk her fill, stretched out on her back and cradled her head in her hands. Matthew ran around the clearing, poking about and discovering butterflies far too big to be real, and black beetles with antlers twice the size of their bodies. James stood, his face wet from the stream, in the centre of the glade, feet apart, back straight, his hands clasping the staff which he had planted firmly before him. There was something quiet, still and unexpectedly threatening about his posture and the way the robe fell severely from him.

In the warm afternoon sun Peter's shadow flickered in all directions, as if searching for something or someone that it had lost. It slowly spread along the ground and covered Wendy, blotting the sun out from her.

Peter stepped over Wendy and stamped his foot against the lower slopes of the mossy bank.

'Come on,' he ordered. 'It's getting late.'

The only answer was a faint jingling which sounded to Wendy more like a real voice than it had before.

Peter crouched down and thrust his head into the earth.

'Come on,' his muffled voice repeated.

'Stupid,' scoffed Tink, contemptuous in the knowledge that Peter could not hear her with his head in the ground.

'What's he doing?' asked Matthew, tugging at James's sleeve. James shrugged.

'No one there,' announced Peter, standing up.

'Where? No one where?' Matthew scampered over to him and ferreted about behind the spray of woodbine that Peter had pushed aside to gain entrance to the Lost Boys' home. 'I can't see anything. What were you – ?' Matthew suddenly disappeared completely.

James sprang from his upright stability and groped after him. Matthew's head popped out of the entrance.

'It's horrid in here,' he said. 'It's dark. And it stinks.' He dragged himself out and rolled down the slope.

'What is it?' asked James. He pushed his head inside for a second, then pulled back quickly with a grimace on his face. 'It does stink.'

'It's our home,' said Peter with as much dignity as he could gather. 'Underground is always a little musty.'

'Let me see,' said Wendy. She left her bed of flowers by the stream and joined them.

'No.'

'Go on.'

'It's too dark for you. It would frighten you.'

'Don't be silly.' Wendy slipped past his outstretched arm and went right into the hole. 'I can't see a thing.'

Peter lingered outside.

'It does smell a little damp,' she said. 'From being underground. But it's not too bad.'

Peter joined her. A light danced around. Tink cast just enough light to let Wendy see.

'How strange,' she said. 'The walls aren't earth at all. What are they?'

'We made them from something we found,' said Peter, 'and covered them with moss and branches so we could be hidden.'

'It's bumpy,' said Wendy.

James and Matthew slid down to them. Matthew was holding his handkerchief over his nose.

'It really does stink.'

'It's cardboard boxes,' said James. 'Opened up and stacked together.'

'Just like the tramps have,' said Matthew.

'Is it?' asked Peter loftily. 'I don't know. We just use what we can find. When they get soggy we make a new house. Then it doesn't smell quite so much,' he added. 'We were just about to move out of this one, actually.'

'What's this on the floor?'

'Oh, just some old things for food.' Peter appeared unconcerned, or he tried to. Children were usually enchanted to be in the Neverland. He didn't remember anyone before being disgusted by the Lost Boys' domestic arrangements.

'Don't you eat berries and fruit?'

'And fresh fish and things?' asked Matthew and James.

'Oh yes. Of course. We eat all that. Yes. But not all the time. We eat other things as well. Things that come in these.' He kicked a pile of rustling wrappers.

'It's chip papers,' said Matthew. 'And burger boxes.'

'I'm going outside,' said James.

Wendy was glad to get out of the foul-smelling hovel but didn't want to upset Peter by saying so. Matthew held a polystyrene box in one hand and a greasy paper bag in the other.

'Where do they come from?' asked James. 'Is that what you eat?'

'Sometimes. We find them in big tubs over there some-where.' Peter waved a lordly finger in a westerly direction.

'But it's junk,' said James. 'You can't say you live off – '

'Where are the others?' asked Wendy hurriedly.

Tink laughed, then shot out of the clearing and out of sight.

'Tink,' Peter shouted. 'Where are they?'

A yell of spiteful rage carried suddenly into the clearing and then the echo of a squealing drill. Matthew began to cry. James looked as though he might be sick. Peter bit his lip and rubbed his side where the pain troubled him. The shadow reared up right into the air as though it had a separate life of its own and a real, solid body. It dropped back to the floor and stretched out across the clearing towards the noise and against the sun.

'Peter,' Wendy called.

Reluctantly he rose up into the air and the others followed. They were high above the bay when they saw the Driller grab the twins and point his swift drill towards them. Peter dived rapidly down towards him, yelling with a scream that froze the children's blood and made Matthew's hair prickle.

There was a fine drizzle in the air when Mr Hacker walked home from the station. He didn't have an umbrella with him so when he got to the front door his hair was plastered to his head and his soggy clothes gave out a musty, unpleasant smell. He always carried a briefcase, but this evening he held a plastic carrier bag in his other hand as well.

'I stopped on the way home,' he explained to his wife, kissing her wetly.

'You're very wet. Slip upstairs and change.'

'Yes. All right. These aren't wet, are they?' he asked anxiously. He handed her the carrier bag. She peered inside.

'No,' she sighed.

'What's wrong?'

'Oh, George.' She blinked tears away.

'Are they the wrong sort?'

She led him to the kitchen. He sighed and nodded. With his three packets there were now five brand-new boxes of breakfast cereal, all different. They were coated in nuts, honey, chocolate and lumps of multi-coloured sugar crystal. They had raisins, dried bananas, bits of apple. They were puffed and they were stretched, they were sticky and they were crunchy.

'I thought they might like a change from muesli,' he said. Mrs Hacker smiled at him unconvincingly. 'They might be back in the morning,' he went on. 'I thought they might even be here now.' And although he knew that they weren't, he peered around the kitchen.

'Have a bath,' his wife encouraged him. 'You're soaking wet and you'll catch cold. Come on.'

He slipped his jacket off and put it on a hanger to dry. Standing in his broad-striped shirt and splendid braces he was glad to be free of the wet coat. His gold cufflinks glinted in the kitchen light. Summer was ending. Already the cars were driving on lights. The kitchen was warm and glowed brightly against the darkening evening sky. Rain trickled down the misted windows. He emptied his loose change from his jacket pockets and found the software program he had slipped in that morning. He turned it over in his hands.

'What's that?'

'Oh, it's something of Matthew's. I might have a go at it later.'

He didn't dress after his bath but wrapped himself in a large dressing gown to eat his dinner. It was a silent meal. Afterwards he took his coffee up to the top of the house. A draught blew unpleasantly from James's open window and the carpet beneath was spattered with raindrops. He wanted to shut it and had to make an effort to stop himself.

He wandered sadly from room to room, touching the beds, looking at the books and pictures. In Matthew's room he sat in front of the computer. He flicked it on and slid the Driller program into the slot. The title scrolled up. He pressed 'Return' and the game started: a line of beach, a row of boulders, a lake, a jungle, a cave mouth, a pool.

His eyes were confused at first by the patterns and symbols. He moved his cursor and a warning bleep sounded. He travelled the shore line of the beach. Something flashed at him from the pool side and the machine buzzed. He moved cautiously nearer. The Driller buzzed again. He pushed the 'fire' button. The Driller edged up the beach away from him along the line of the row of boulders. He fired again. The Driller buzzed louder. Another close shot. The Driller darted the last few feet of beach and escaped into the cave. Mr Hacker hesitated, then followed.

As soon as his cursor entered the black mouth of the cave, the screen blacked out. A network of tunnels appeared, a maze of traps and tricks and dead ends. Here and there small orange glows of fire threatened. He inched slowly forward. Where was the Driller? What were those squat, clumsy shapes that moved so confidently through the dark labyrinth? He turned a corner. The gentle buzzing suddenly switched to a fierce squeal. The screen went white.

```
GAME OVER
PLAYER DRILLED
20 POINTS
```

'Stop!' the Driller screamed through flashing steel teeth. His mouth gaped open with delight at the chase. Peter swooped over his head and reared up again. The Driller, his arm tight around the twins' necks, pointed the squealing drill at their faces.

'Back!' he shouted. 'Or they're finished.'

'Coward!' Peter yelled.

'Come to my little home in the cave and say that.' The Driller laughed. He edged his way along the line of the boulders towards the black mouth of the cave, dragging the terrified twins with him.

'Leave them alone.'

'Oh no. No, no, no. They're hungry. And they're ill. That loutish boy said so. The one with his hands in his pockets. He said they needed looking after. Driller will look after them.' The drill had dropped to a low buzz.

Peter zoomed up and down, following the Driller, but keeping his distance.

'Put them down,' he shouted. 'Put them down and fight me.'

'Oh yes?' The Driller had been tricked before. 'You'll fly away.'

'I won't.'

'Will.'

'Won't.'

'Liar.'

Peter dropped to the beach. His feet kicked the fine sand.

'Come on, then. Put them down.'

The Driller was at the cave mouth.

'Later.' His voice echoed from the lip of the cave. 'Later. When I choose. And on my terms.' He slipped out of sight into the stinking maze.

Mr Hacker flicked off the computer. The screen died.

'Come to bed,' said his wife.

'All right.'

They looked into the children's rooms together.

'They've gone without shoes,' he said.

'Yes.'

'I hope they're all right.'

Faces popped out of the jungle round the bay. Faces painted with shock and distress.

Peter flew away from the cave, back to Matthew and James and Wendy. He raised an arm and gestured to the Lost Boys.

'It's him,' said Matthew.

The others nodded.

'Did you see his hair?'

'Yes.'

'Red.'

'Yes.'

'And the scar. And the moustache.'

'Yes.'

'I told you.'

'The drill,' said Wendy. 'It was horrid.'

'Did you hear it?' asked Matthew. 'Buzzz.'

'Shut up,' Peter ordered.

'Buzzz.'

Peter slapped Matthew's face. 'Shut up.'

Matthew fell to the floor and thrashed his legs about and screamed.

'I didn't hurt him,' Peter protested quickly.

Looter was intrigued. 'What have you done to him?'

'It's a tantrum,' James explained. 'He isn't hurt.'

'Just doing it?' asked Looter.

'Yes.'

'It's horrible,' said Bins. 'Can't he stop?'

'Not till he's ready,' said James. 'He just gets worse if you try to stop him.'

'Oh,' said Looter. He swung his foot back and kicked Matthew in the stomach. Matthew stopped screaming.

'There you are,' said Looter, with a smile. 'Stopped.'

'He can't breathe,' said Bins.

Looter shrugged. 'He's breathing a bit. It's a bit jerky, but he's breathing. He *could* scream if he wanted.'

'You can't do that,' said James. 'He's only seven.'

'Too old for tantrums,' said Looter. 'Isn't he?'

'You leave him alone or . . .'

'You want him to scream?' asked Colin.

'No.'

'Well, he's shut up.'

James dropped his staff and swung a fist at Looter, but the Lost Boy stepped back and James lost his footing in the sand. Peter picked up the staff very carefully and handed it to James as though he were frightened of it.

'You'd better hold on to this. It might be useful.'

James took it and noticed for the first time since they had been in the Neverland that the staff felt rougher and heavier than it had before. He put out a hand and pulled Matthew up. Matthew's face was red but he wasn't crying and he was breathing steadily again.

'I don't like it here,' said Matthew, tugging at James's hand. 'Let's go home.'

Wendy was very pale. James wasn't sure whether she was very angry or very frightened.

'I don't think we can,' she said to Peter. 'Can we?'

'No.'

'Why?' wailed Matthew.

'Because of them,' said Wendy. She pointed to the cave.

'Who are they?'

'They looked like twins,' she said.

Peter nodded. 'Samneric.'

'Lost Boys?'

'Yes.'

'And these?'

Peter surveyed the bedraggled group. 'That's all of them.'

They stared at Wendy. She held out her hand. 'How do you do? I'm Wendy. This is James, and this is Matthew.'

Bins took her hand and shook it violently. Then he started to wheeze and rattle. He blew his coughing over Wendy's face so she had to turn her head aside and take her hand away.

'What's up?' asked James.

'Ass-mar,' he groaned. 'Ass—' The rest disappeared in another fit of spluttering. He staggered away and sat at the poolside with his back to them.

'His name's Bins,' said Peter. 'He wandered off from school one day because everyone made fun of him for being so fat and for wearing specs and for coughing. He got lost trying to get home.'

'A Lost Boy,' said Matthew.

'They're all Lost Boys. This one,' he pointed to the very thin boy, 'this one's Hardly. His mum ran off and he lived with his sister and his dad. His dad knocked them about a lot so he ran off with his sister. But in the end she didn't want him either, so he was lost.'

'Hello, Hardly,' said Wendy.

Hardly hung his head, ashamed of his story. He felt that it was his fault that both his mother and his sister had deserted him. He felt guilty that his father had hit him so badly.

'Colin,' said Peter, pointing to the boy with the pocked face, 'was moved out of his house and put in a flat right at the top of a tower block. He hated it. One day he went back to where he used to live and they had driven huge machines over it all, roads, shops, houses, pubs, everything was gone. It was all heaps of brick and rubble. He walked all over it trying to find his old house but he never could. Then it got dark and he was lost.'

Colin dragged something through his throat and spat into the pool defiantly. The parrot fish hung heavily from his hands, its colours fading in death. He threw it away.

'This is Looter,' Peter went on. 'He . . .'

'I'll tell her,' said Looter. 'I bunked off school every day.'

'Why?' asked James.

'Don't be stupid.'

'Oh.'

'I bunked off and went down the arcades. Played the machines all the time.'

'Didn't you need a lot of money for that?' asked Wendy.

Looter looked shy and triumphant both at the same time.

'Easy. I knocked things off from the shops. Alarm clocks, sweets, stockings, anything. I sold them in the arcades and put the money in the machines.'

'Didn't they make you go back to school?' asked Matthew. He thought Looter sounded the best of the Lost Boys, even though he'd kicked him. He wished he could show him his computer and the Driller game. With a sick feeling in his stomach he remembered that he didn't have to. He remembered that he had only to lift his eyes to the end of the row of boulders to see the mouth of the cave where the real Driller was hiding, with the two boys he had captured.

'Make me?' sneered Looter. 'They couldn't make me. Anyway, they didn't want to. They liked it better when I wasn't there.'

I bet they did, thought James. He wondered if Looter had really got any hands, or if his arms ended where his wrists were always thrust into his pockets.

'So I played the machines all the time. I got so good I could go on for hours on just one go. Then one day it didn't seem worth going home so I stayed in the arcade. Then I forgot how to get home if I wanted to, and I was lost.'

'I see,' said Wendy politely. 'Thank you very much.'

'Where's your crab?' Looter asked Bins. The fat boy had stopped coughing.

'Dropped it in the jungle. It crawled off.'

How dirty they all look, thought Wendy. And how tired.

'What will happen to them?' asked James.

'Who?' Peter was thinking of something else.

'Those twins. The ones the Driller took away.'

'Samneric,' said Bins helpfully.

'What a funny name. Who are they?' asked Wendy.

'Don't know. They've always been here.'

'In the Neverland?'

'Suppose so.'

'But they must have come from somewhere. How did they get lost?'

'Let's get going,' said Looter. 'It's getting dark.'

The sun had dipped down and was hanging just above the line of jungle to the west of the bay. The children all had long shadows rolled out behind them, all except Peter. His shadow was longer than the rest and stretched out at right angles to the others, pointing towards the cave and the Driller.

'I wish it wouldn't do that,' said James. 'Can't you make it go the right way, like ours?'

'You must remember them arriving,' said Wendy. 'You were here first.'

'They just walked in one day across the sand. They said they came out of the jungle. They said they didn't have any mother.'

'The Driller will be out again soon,' warned Looter. 'Soon as it's dark.'

'Everyone has a mother,' Matthew argued.

'Not Samneric. They were in a book. The man who wrote it wanted them for one little bit, then, when it was finished, he didn't need them any more so he just left them.'

'Where?'

'In the jungle. On the beach. Lost.'

'We can't go back,' said Colin.

'Why not?' Bins was getting anxious. His eyes kept going to the cave. He moved nearer to Wendy.

'They'll tell him.'

'Colin's right,' agreed Looter. 'Samneric will tell Driller where we live. He'll come when we're asleep and . . .'

'Buzzz,' said Colin.

Bins put his hand into Wendy's. He was smelly but she didn't like to turn her head away.

'Don't,' said Hardly.

'We'll find somewhere,' said Peter. 'Come on.'

'Where?' asked James.

'Anywhere. Into the jungle. Come on.'

They pushed the heavy leaves aside and took a narrow path, almost invisible, it was so grown over. Beneath the clenched fist of the trees the darkness thickened.

# Seven

THE Driller dragged the twins roughly down the hot tunnels underneath the cave. The stench was quite unlike anything they had ever known before. At first they thought they would not be able to breathe in the foul air, but as their bodies were jolted and jarred by the Driller's hurtling descent into the labyrinth they gasped in pain and terror and dragged the stinking atmosphere into their lungs.

The tunnels sloped down sharply. With every swift step the Driller plunged deeper into the earth beneath the Neverland. The darkness was so complete that they could not see that at every few paces the tunnels forked and turned. There were tunnels leading into blind alleys and dead ends, tunnels leading to different parts of the intricate network of caves, tunnels leading to pit openings that would hurtle an ignorant traveller deep into the fiery heart of the Neverland. The Driller never paused. He ran backwards dragging his captives with him in a confident path to the place he had in mind.

Still holding hands, the twins whimpered in fear but he clenched his arm tighter around their necks. 'Shut up,' he snapped through his steel teeth. It seemed impossible to them that he should know where he was in the darkness, but the Driller's eyes were just as good in light and dark. It was as clear to him in the tunnels as on the beach in the afternoon sun.

They turned yet another corner. The twins banged against the sharp edge. Then the Driller slowed down. The twins could make out the shape of his face. Their heads were bent so far back that he glowered down into their eyes. He stopped and flung them to the floor.

Shaken by the journey, rattled with panic and shock, they clung to one another. They moved cautiously away.

'Don't roll too far from Driller,' he said, laughing. 'Look out.' He shot his hand out and grabbed a twin by the ankle. 'Look.' He lifted them and let them see that they had been crawling towards a gaping pit that dropped miles down into the fires beneath. The orange glow that had lit the Driller's face for them came from the flames. 'Now then, my dears.' He smiled with steel teeth. 'Driller wants to visit your home in the jungle.'

Peter, Wendy, James, Matthew and the Lost Boys walked straight through the clearing with the Lost Boys' old home in it. Hardly looked longingly at the woodbine arched over the hidden entrance. He was tired and hungry.

'Where are we going?' he asked.

'It doesn't matter,' said Peter. 'As long as we don't stay here.'

'The twins won't tell.'

'They might be dead,' Colin called.

'No.'

Overhead, Tink jangled out a warning. 'Don't trust the Driller. He'll come looking.'

'Shut up, Tink. It's your fault we've got to do this.'

The Lost Boys had told Peter Tink's story about the food.

Tink flew off grumbling.

'Press on,' Peter urged. 'It's nearly pitch dark.'

They crashed through the undergrowth on the other side of the clearing. Even Peter could hardly see any path now. He really was very angry with Tink for her stupid trick that had led to the capture of the twins but he was too tired to chase her and the pain was getting much worse now.

'I'm stopping here,' said Matthew suddenly. He sat down by the side of the path. The jungle floor was soft and squashy. A little pool of water immediately formed where he had depressed the earth. The seat of his pyjamas was soaked. He opened his mouth wide to scream.

'Don't,' said Looter.

Matthew leaped to his feet. 'I'm all right,' he said.

Looter looked shyly at him. He took one hand out of his pocket and put it down to Matthew. 'Come on,' he said. 'Stay with me.'

Matthew smiled up at the bigger boy and squeezed his hand. It was comforting to be led through the dusk but there was something odd about Looter's grip.

The heavy undergrowth thinned out. Gaps appeared between the trees. The air grew less humid and oppressive. A gentle breeze pushed through the trees and refreshed them a little. It was difficult to tell in the growing dark, but it looked as if the trees were taller, more upright, less twisted and stunted than they had been earlier. Peter stooped, bent down, ran his hand over the ground and found his fingers brushing against dry pine needles. He sniffed, identifying at last the fragrant scent of the resin from the trees that had been teasing their nostrils for a few paces.

'This will do,' he said. 'We'll sleep here.'

The Lost Boys and the others fell gratefully to the forest floor. Matthew was asleep in seconds. Looter lay beside him, one arm across his shoulders for protection. Bins curled into a ball and slept. Hardly crept to a bush and hid beside it. Colin leaned back against a tree and patted his pockets looking for a last cigarette but he fell asleep before he found one.

'Keep a guard, Tink,' Peter ordered. He lay on the pine needles, rubbing the pain in his side.

'Go to sleep, Wendy,' said James.

'Yes, I'm tired.'

James was surprised to find that he was not ready for sleep. He stood, feet apart, hands clasped on his staff which was planted firmly in front of him. He stayed for an hour silently keeping guard before he too slept. Tink flew off to find something more interesting to do.

Among the trees, silent eyes watched and waited. They saw Tink disappear. They saw James lie down next to his staff and close his eyes.

'They're all asleep now.'

'Yes.'

Mrs Hacker turned over in her sleep and moaned. It woke her husband. He looked at the clock. Half past three.

'What is it?'

'Nothing.'

'I heard a noise.'

'Are they back?'

He checked their rooms while she sat up in bed remembering her bad dream.

'No. Beds empty.'

'Yes.'

'You moaned.'

'Did I?'

'Why?'

'Oh, George. The eyes. All around them.'

'What eyes?'

'I don't know.'

He put his arm round her.

'It's all right.'

'Is it?'

The twins listened fearfully to the strange sounds echoing around the huge cavern lit by the hot glow from the underground fire. The pit itself gave out deep boomings from time to time, like distant thunder. The Driller paced up and down, his feet crunching the gravelly floor. At first they thought he was humming tunelessly to himself, but gradually they realised with sick feelings in their stomachs that the low noise was from the drill at his right wrist. All the time it turned slowly. From further off, beyond where the light helped their eyes, shuffles and slow panting sounds crept towards them. They were gurgly and wet, a huge monster with a very unpleasant cold. At intervals a rasping sound was followed by a yelp. The twins did not know it but this was because Jooks let his wet troll's mouth loll open into a snore. This woke Strakey who kicked him and made him yelp. Most trolls snore. They sleep in caverns heated from the fire pits but they don't like the light so they roll into dank corners.

Samneric looked around to see where these horrid noises were coming from, but their eyes could not pierce beyond the flickering orange glow.

The Driller stopped pacing and stood still, his body tense, his head erect.

'Cheko. Loder,' he called. 'Strakey. Jooks.' The ugly names boomed around the great space. 'Slee. Skylights. Come on. Night's here. Time for some dirty work.' His moustache lifted under the movement of the cruel smile. The twins gazed horror-struck as Slee shuffled into the firelight, his hands scraping the floor.

'Skylights is dead,' he said.

'What?'

'You drilled him. Yesterday.'

The twins tightened their grip on one another.

Cheko and Loder moved into the light. Loder lifted his ugly head and sniffed. It was a dreadful sound, wet and

gurgly. He did it again. He cocked his great broad head questioningly.

'Yes,' said the Driller. 'Over by the fire.'

The troll's mouth gaped open in a delighted grin. Strings of spit stretched between his rubbery lips. He made clumsy little dancing movements. The other trolls heard the Driller's news as they reached the group and they all turned their faces towards the fire and the twins. They screwed their eyes up. Although the glow was only dim it was painful to the trolls and they could not make out the twins. Loder giggled and the twins gasped when they saw him bend his arms round so that he could clap his hands together. This is not at all easy to do when your hands are fixed on back to front and it looked very frightening.

'No, Loder,' the Driller snapped.

Loder stopped clapping. 'Why?'

'We need them.'

'How many?'

'Two. Thin ones. Not much meat on them.'

Loder shuffled uncomfortably. 'Little ones are sweet.'

The twins thought they were going to faint.

'No. We're not eating them. Not tonight.'

'When?'

'Later. Perhaps.'

The Driller did not like trolls. He only spoke to them because they were bad. He needed their help to fight Peter and the Lost Boys, but he hated the way they always wanted to eat people. He thought it was nasty. And they were so dirty. He thought sorrowfully about the mess his lovely, broad-striped shirt must be in after the crazy dash through the slimy trolls' tunnels. He lifted an arm to look, and the heavy gold cufflinks glinted in the firelight.

'They smell good,' said Loder.

'Remember Skylights,' the Driller warned and the low hum increased to a threatening buzz.

'Now then, boys,' he went on. 'Show these two little ones what you can do.'

He strode over to the twins.

'You needn't try to escape. Beyond there,' he motioned expansively with his left hand, 'is a maze of tunnels, all sin black in their darkness. Once you stray in there you'll never come out. You'll be lost for ever. Understand?'

The twins nodded.

A mumbled message came over from Slee.

'What's that?' asked the Driller.

'The beasts. The others.'

'Yes. I was coming to that. And there are all sorts of things down there that make my boys look like angels of glory. There are slimy things that wriggle and sting; crawly things as big as a man but with fifteen legs; wobbly things that spread all over you so you disappear into them – and more, lots more. Whatever you can imagine, whatever creeps into your dreams at night and wakes you in terror from your sleep. They're all down my tunnels, and if you run off you'll meet them, but this time they're real and you won't wake up.'

The trolls were laughing.

'So you won't run away on your own, will you, my dears?'

The twins shook their heads.

'And you'll help Driller?' he cooed. 'We want a nice party for you and all your friends. Don't we, boys?'

More gurgles of stupid, greedy laughter came from the trolls.

'That's right. A little party at your friends' house. Me and the boys and you.'

'We won't,' said Samneric together. 'We won't take you.'

'Yes you will.' The Driller smiled, baring his steel teeth. 'Look and see. See how you take my boys to find the little house in the jungle.'

He dragged the twins to their feet and began to pull them back towards the beach. The trolls surged round them, backs bent, axes lifted from the tunnel floor.

'My boys will do it. Now we've got you. My boys can do it.'

'We can. We can,' the trolls joined in, their stinking breath chanting it out.

The cold moon shone down from a clear sky and then back up again from the still pool. The Driller marched the twins over to the rocky edge.

'Now, boys,' he shouted.

One by one the trolls came up and ran their hideous faces and huge wet noses over the twins, smearing them with foul mucus. Then they dropped their heads and bent their backs so that their noses hung just above the ground. They sniffed around.

'Got it?' asked the Driller.

They bayed excitedly.

'I take it you did come from your little hiding place yesterday?' he asked.

'No,' they lied.

He laughed.

'Well, let's see, shall we. Off, boys. Off.'

The trolls sniffed up the beach, into the jungle and along the path towards the Lost Boys' underground house. The Driller forced the twins along in front of him.

'Home. Home. Come along, little dears. We're going home.'

The moon cast a line of silver across the rippling surface of the lake, stretching from the beach to the palm grove at the edge of the Great Sand Wastes. By day the sun tortured the sands and anyone who dared to walk across them. As soon as the moon rose and the darkness gathered, the sand gave up its heat and the night air whipped chill over the flowing ridges. Travellers pitched camp and huddled for warmth in their robes.

Horses and camels were tied beneath the palms. Three tents pointed their fingers into the night sky. These were not flimsy campers' tents, cheap and nasty. They were a portable palace. In one, the biggest, food was prepared, clothes stored and cared for, servants chattered in the evening and slept at night. Two more, rather smaller, were the court apartments of Prince Ali and his sisters the princesses Rahila and Amina. Huge cushions, richly embroidered and intricately patterned, furnished the sisters' tent. Rich carpets hung from the sides, keeping out draughts and delighting the eye. To one side an iron stove gave safe heat, allowing the three royal children to cast off heavy cloaks and sit at ease in light flowing silks and cottons. Ali and Amina drank sherbet; Rahila sipped a glass of sweet mint tea.

'Not tonight,' she said. 'I'm too tired.'

'You must,' Amina insisted. Rahila, at thirteen, was the oldest. Ali tried to boss her about because although he was only ten she was only a girl. He thought she should do what he said. In this opinion he was just like James and Wendy. Rahila sometimes let him think he was in charge, but if anything important happened she usually made the decisions.

'Oh, must I?' She laughed at Amina. The little girl's face fell. Nine-year-olds do not like to be laughed at. It is something they often grow out of by the time they are about ninety but not always.

'Yes, you must,' ordered Ali, joining in. 'I insist.'

This was very difficult for Rahila. She wanted to do it now for Amina so that she should not be disappointed, but she did not want to do anything if Ali ordered her to.

'All right,' she decided. 'Shall it be a new one or an old one?'

'New,' demanded Amina.

'Old,' Ali ordered.

'Good.' Rahila clapped her hands. 'So it shall be new. Are you ready?'

Amina's delighted head nodded. Ali's rather serious one kept still. Now he would have to stay and listen to a new story against his instructions or show his disapproval by going to his own tent. He stayed.

Most nights, Rahila told her brother and sister a story at bedtime. Sometimes it was best to hear a favourite old one, sometimes it was exciting to hear a new one. Rahila sat quite still for several minutes while the story was born in her mind. A servant came in, silently gathered up the empty cups and glasses, placed a small tray of very sticky, very sweet morsels on a carved table and went out walking backwards. The tent flap closed behind her. Across the sand the chatter of other servants carried from their big tent. A horse whinnied. The palm fronds rustled an impatient warning overhead.

'Right,' announced Rahila. 'This is it. The sea rippled and danced in the moonlight. Overhead the children flew in over the beach.'

'That's stupid,' interrupted Ali. 'Children don't fly.'

'These had been given power by a great djinn,' said Rahila.

'Why didn't you say so?'

Rahila glared at him. 'Much goes on in stories that needs no explanation.' She thought for a second. 'They circled the beach and set off over the jungle.'

Amina and Ali lost themselves in Rahila's story. She wondered at herself as the strange tale unfolded in her head.

Far away, in a clearing in the forest, children slept. Soft, delicate feet trod the ground around them. Low voices exchanged views.

'We should wake them. Do it now.'

'No. Let them alone.'

'Why?'

'We can watch them all the time. They won't go away if we don't want them to.'

'We should act quickly. Take them.'

'No. Wait.'

There was the shuffling sound of steel being drawn from a scabbard. A bright sword flashed in the moonlight.

'Do you see his staff?'

'Yes.'

'And his robes?'

'Of course.'

'It means trouble.'

'Danger.'

'Trolls.'

'We don't want it.'

'No.'

'Wait. We'll wait.'

All night the wide eyes watched through the branches.

The Driller snarled in fury. The cardboard house was empty. He kicked the soggy corrugations to pieces, danced furiously on the grave of their house.

The trolls found the clearing with no difficulty. Their slimy nostrils were alive to every detail of scent that was different from their own sweaty foulness. Slee sidled up to the Driller, keeping on his left, away from the angry drill.

'This way,' he said.

'What's that?'

'Look.'

Slee buried his head in a pile of twisted cardboard. 'Got one,' he sniffed. 'A different one.' He kept his head low and followed the scent to a path from the clearing.

'Follow!' bayed the Driller. 'After them!'

They crashed through the stinging leaves and tendrils, chasing round and through the jungle. The Driller dragged the twins with him, locked in his strong grip.

Cheko lagged behind, sniffing carefully. He thought the scent was stronger on a different path from the clearing. He stood for a long time, his simple face screwed up in the nearest he could get to thought. Surely it was stronger here? Did that mean it was the last path they took? It was too difficult for a troll and he did not like being in the jungle on his own so he turned from the path and followed the others.

When he caught them up they were on the beach again, gathered at the pool.

'Fool!' screamed the Driller, prodding his drill at Slee. 'Stupid fool!'.

Poor Slee stood with his feet turned in, toes touching, his heavy axe dangling from thick fingers.

The Driller shouted at him for a long time, his right arm waving in front of the troll's face. He screamed terrible threats. At last Cheko was able to explain about the stronger scent.

'Right,' the Driller said. 'Try again.'

But the sky to the east of the cove was already splashed with pink and orange. Soon the rim of the sun would lift above the horizon and the trolls would stumble in blind pain. It was time to go back to the tunnels.

'Tomorrow,' said the Driller grimly. He pointed the whining drill straight between Slee's eyes. 'And you'd better hope the scent's still strong in the morning or it's the pit for you.' Slee nodded. 'Here,' the Driller snapped. 'Take these back.' He flung the twins at the trolls.

Back in the huge cavern, where the fire boomed below them, Samneric fell into a deep exhausted sleep.

The Driller never slept. He spent the day pacing the beach. He washed his shirt and hung it on a bough to dry. He watched the crocodile make its daily journey to the wounded ship. And he waited for night and the hunt.

# *Eight*

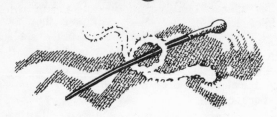

T HE trolls shuffled off into their dark corners. Loder threw something nasty to the twins.

'Eat.' He disappeared into the gloom.

'It's horrible,' said Sam, or it might have been Eric.

'It's slimy,' said Eric, or it might have been Sam.

They put it to their lips. It was so bad that they gagged, but then hunger overcame disgust and they crammed it into their mouths.

'What do you suppose it is?'

'Don't ask.'

Daylight never penetrated the trolls' caves. The first rays of the sun that lit up the broad stripes of the Driller's shirt, swaying in a light breeze, were locked out from Samneric. Full from the disgusting food and exhausted by the night's hunt, they huddled together and fell asleep.

Mrs Hacker turned over in bed and reached out a hand for her husband.

'George?'

She was alone.

'George?' Louder.

She flung off the duvet and crossed the room. Noises

of shots being fired, bleeping and zooming, crackling and hissing drifted down the stairs. A siren wailed.

'Oh, blast!' shouted her husband. There was an explosion, then silence. He slouched down to her in a dressing gown and a bad mood.

'He escaped.'

'Where?'

'Into the tunnels. I was right behind him when he jumped me.'

'Oh, George.'

'Drilled me through.'

Rahila stood by the lakeside enjoying the morning coolness before the sun rose high in the sky and lit the furnace of light that blazed all day over the desert. She raised her arms above her head and ran her hands through her long black hair. The breeze from the lake lifted it from her shoulders and sent it streaming behind her. She was free and cool. Hearing footsteps dragging through the sand behind her she dropped her arms and covered the lower half of her face with a veil.

'Are we moving on today?' asked Ali.

'What do you think?' Decisions were always easier if it looked as though her brother made them.

'I don't mind. It would be good to stay here for a few days. Ride a little, perhaps. Fish. Exercise Khan.' He lifted an arm to display the splendid hooded falcon on his wrist.

'Good. We'll stay.'

The bird raised its feathers, shook the slender leather jesses on its scaly legs. The beautiful plumage settled back into sleek perfection. Beneath the leather hood the bird's eyes stared into darkness. Ali smiled proudly at his sister. Her returned smile pleased him, made him more proud than ever of his fine bird. He raised himself to his full height so that he was only a couple of inches shorter than Rahila, and put a confident hand to the hilt of the broad, curved scimitar tucked into his waistband.

'We'll get some fresh meat. Rabbit. Won't we, Khan?'

The bird lifted one foot, talons open, ready to seize its prey.

Wendy stretched out a palm, clutched something in her sleep, clenched her fist and found it full of needles. She opened her eyes and looked in wonder at her hand. Bringing it to her nose she smelled the aromatic resin. The pine needles tumbled through her fingers. Confusion cleared in her head. She remembered where she was. She looked around. James was standing in that strange attitude she had never seen him use before but which had become his custom, in the Neverland. All the others were asleep.

'James.'

He turned, looking distant for a moment as though his sister were a stranger, then smiled. She went over to him.

'Is it all right?'

'I'm not sure. I thought I saw something move. In the trees.'

He pointed with his staff. They both looked, but there was nothing.

'Have you been awake all night?'

He shook his head.

'The birds woke me.'

For the first time Wendy became aware of the deep-throated calling of many birds, filling the glade.

'Let's get the others up.'

In the trees two slender figures turned their eyes to each other.

'Did you see him point the wand?'

'Yes.'

'It's him.'

'It must be,'

They went off to discuss it.

Wendy and James shook the others gently to wake them. Colin pulled his half-smoked cigarette out of his pocket and started to pat his clothes looking for matches.

'No,' said Wendy. She took the dog-end from him and crumpled it up, letting the dry tobacco fall among the pine needles.

'Here,' objected Colin.

'No more of that,' said Wendy.

Colin slouched away moodily. He made a noise in his throat, getting ready to spit.

'And you can stop that. No more spitting.'

Colin muttered something. Wendy could just hear it and knew that it was an absolutely dreadful word, but she decided to ignore it for the moment. Smoking and spitting were quite enough to deal with on the first morning. Swearing would come later.

'This is lovely,' she said to Peter. 'Where are we?'

He shrugged. 'I don't know.'

'There's blackberries,' said Hardly. 'Look.' He was offering two cupped hands, full of plump juicy berries. His smile looked broader and happier than before because of the way his teeth contrasted with the blue juice around his lips.

'And nuts,' said Bins. 'Walnuts.'

'You've never been here before?' Wendy asked.

'No.'

'It's not like the jungle,' said Matthew. 'But I like it.'

'Look over there,' called James.

They joined him by a stream that ran through the woods just past the clearing. Patches of sunlight fell into the stony bottom. In the shaded areas fat brown trout shimmered lazily.

'Make a fire,' said James. 'Trout for breakfast.'

Autumn leaves glowed gold on the trees above them, ready to fall as soon as the first wind of winter cut through the wood. The boys ran around snapping dry branches and piling them up on a heap of pine needles. All the trees Wendy had ever seen were there. Not just the tall, elegant pines with their armoured cones, but great beeches, hung with scaly nuts, spreading oaks, horse chestnuts carved with conkers, and more delicate Spanish chestnuts with ripe fruit curled up in spiny cases, tiny hedgehogs. As she thought this a real hedgehog tiptoed, back arched, past her feet.

'Oh,' she said. 'Lovely.'

Colin lit the fire with his matches. The trout were perfect, sweet, with a slightly muddy flavour from the bottom of the stream.

'They just swim into your hands,' Looter said happily, crumbling a piece of scorched skin in his mouth.

'We've gone too far,' moaned Peter. 'It's not Neverland.'

'It must be,' argued Wendy.

'I don't know it.'

'That's because we've never been here before. It's our Neverland. James's and Matthew's and mine.'

'No.'

'Of course.'

'The Neverland's mine,' said Peter.

'I don't think so,' said James. 'I think all children make the Neverland, but the ones who come here make it most. It's always changing.'

Peter grimaced and put his hand to his side.

'Does it hurt?' asked Wendy.

'No.' He looked puzzled. 'No.'

'Then why are you rubbing it?'

Peter made no answer although she wished he would. She looked long and hard at him, thinking how small he was, how thin, and how she wished she could cuddle him and look after him. Just then, his shadow leaped from its proper place and slapped on to her face. It was only a shadow so it could not hurt her, but the darkness changed her expression and she let her eyes fall.

A sudden chattering from a tree above made them look up in alarm. A chimpanzee swang from the horse-chestnut tree, lobbed a coconut at the children and swung off. After their surprise they all laughed.

'You see,' said James. 'It is the Neverland.'

'Whose chimp was that?' asked Bins.

'Mine, I think,' said Matthew. 'I liked the jungle.'

'I think this is better,' decided Wendy. 'Not so wet. Not so hot. More like home.'

So it was. The sun was full in the sky, but instead of burning down into the steamy jungle it spread a comforting early-autumn warmth through the forest glade.

'Let's live here,' said Bins, eager to please Wendy. 'Always.'

'Let's build a home,' said Hardly.

'Can't. No cardboard,' Colin objected.

'Don't need cardboard, do we? Don't like cardboard.'

'Pine branches,' said James.

Wendy had other plans for the Lost Boys, but she thought it would be a good idea for them to build somewhere to sleep in so she did not object. The sleep and the good breakfast had refreshed them all. They bounded away and stripped broad dark-green pine branches from the lower parts of the trees where they spread out like thick fans. It was hard and messy work. The sap bled out from the jagged wounds where the boughs were torn from the trunk. Peter allowed Matthew, James and the Lost Boys to do most of it while he flew around, stopping every now and then to hew off a stubborn branch with his sharp dagger.

'Come on. Hurry up. Don't just twist that about, let me slash it off. Give a big pull. All together.' Peter had an endless store of advice and encouragement.

There was soon a magnificent pile of sturdy branches thick with needles that would make a magnificent shelter. But, every time they tried to erect them into a secure arrangement the weight of the boughs grew too heavy for the simple architecture and they tumbled in.

'It's rubbish,' said Colin. He kicked the heap of branches and slouched off.

Poor Hardly had worked harder than anyone and was

worn out. Bins had been so excited and pleased that he had forgotten to be ill, but now that the house would not stand up his face blushed a deep red and he started to gasp.

'Can't do no more,' he wheezed. 'My ass-mar.' He waddled off and sank to the ground.

Looter had done very little. He kept his hands in his pockets most of the time. If there was a really heavy branch he thrust his hand deep into the foliage and helped to drag it into place. Matthew hung around near to him. He tried once or twice to hold his hand but Looter shook his head. Matthew drifted away. 'No, it's all right,' said Looter. 'I just don't want to hold hands.' He smiled down at Matthew. 'Stay here.' Matthew grinned happily. They chatted for a long time about computer games while the others worked. Now they stood together looking at the pile of useless branches.

'It needs something strong to hold it up in the middle,' said Looter.

They tried to get a thick straight branch and trim the leaves from it, but even Peter's dagger would not cut through anything suitable. It was hopeless.

'Forget it,' said Peter. 'We'll sleep in the open again, like last night.'

Wendy was upset to see that all the enthusiasm and happiness that had made the Lost Boys look so much better was turning to disappointment. They were all looking ill again.

'There must be some way,' she urged.

'What about that?' Looter asked. He lifted a hand from his pocket and pointed at James's staff.

'No,' said James quickly. 'Not this.'

'It's just right,' crowed Peter. He soared into the air with joy and dive-bombed James, grabbing at the staff.

'Your hand!' shouted Matthew. Wendy looked at Looter's pointing finger.

Peter shrieked. James lifted his staff high and swung it

round, flinging Peter through the clearing and into the trees. He banged against a huge elm and dropped to the floor.

Looter stuffed his hands back into his pockets and ran over to Peter.

'His hands are on back to front,' hissed Matthew at Wendy. 'Did you see?'

Wendy nodded.

Peter did not move.

'You've knocked him out,' said Matthew.

'It's bad,' said Hardly.

'I didn't do anything,' protested James.

'Did,' said Colin. He started to get ready to spit, but then he caught Wendy's eye and stopped himself.

'He grabbed my staff,' argued James.

'Swung him round,' said Colin.

'Never seen anything like it,' Hardly added.

'Right into the tree. Wallop,' wheezed Bins.

'Not right,' said Colin.

'Look –' shouted James.

'It's all right,' said Wendy. 'But we've got to look after him.'

'Put him under cover,' said Looter.

'Right. Can't leave him out here,' Colin agreed. 'Give us your stick.'

For a moment James and Colin stared at each other defiantly. Then James nodded. 'Come on then,' he said. He strode over to the heap of branches. Clasping his staff with both hands he drove it into the ground. It went straight down, like a drill. When James let go, the staff was firm and upright. In no time at all the branches were leaned against it, lashed together to make an elegant shelter. Then they all crawled in and lay, tired and perplexed. Looter ignored Matthew and huddled in a corner. He was surprised to feel a small hand slip through his arm. He looked down to see Matthew's little face smiling up at him.

'It doesn't matter,' whispered Matthew.

Looter grunted.

'Please will you hold my hand?' Matthew asked him.

Looter opened his palm to Matthew. They rested side by side and happy.

In the cove, the Driller furrowed his brow. His shirt was dry now and he shrugged it over his strong shoulders. It was hard work getting the gold links into the cuffs but he managed it with his one hand and his steel teeth. He felt better once he was properly dressed. How to find where the Lost Boys were, he wondered. Would the scent be strong enough?

Wendy was disturbed by a movement. The Lost Boys and her brothers were napping in the shelter in the early afternoon. Wendy stepped out to look around the glade and plan the next move. It was difficult without Peter. Her eyes were caught by a dark shimmering at the edge of the little pine house. It grew in size. Indistinct at first, it gradually became clear that a whole shadow was slipping out of the shelter. Wendy stiffened and watched. Peter's perfect silhouette was lying on the ground looking as if it was wondering what to do next. It had escaped. It moved hesitantly one way, then stopped. It tried another direction. In a flash it darted over the forest floor and leaped on Wendy. She felt a sick feeling in her stomach and a stabbing pain in her side. Her head went dizzy.

It left her as suddenly as it had come. The shadow slipped off her and hurled itself across the glade and into the forest and disappeared.

# Nine

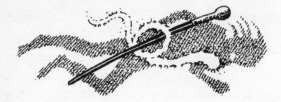

MATTHEW called from inside the shelter. Wendy fled across the glade and into the green gloom of its branches. Peter lay very still and calm. The boys formed a circle around him.

'He mumbled something about it hurting,' said James.

'Then he moved a lot, like a tantrum,' said Matthew.

'Then he fell into a deep sleep,' Hardly added.

'He seems all right now.'

'I think he will be, for a while,' said Wendy. But she wondered whether Peter needed his shadow in order to get better again. His face looked peaceful and happy, happier than she had ever seen it before.

'Come on,' she said briskly. 'Time to get on.'

'What?' asked Colin.

'Good-oh,' Matthew chattered and he tugged Looter out into the afternoon light.

'All in a row,' ordered Wendy. 'Let's look at you.'

They shuffled into line.

'You're filthy,' said Wendy.

Tink saw the shadow hurtling through the jungle. In a flash and a jangle she was after it. She darted through the air. They both travelled at top speed, reaching the beach in minutes. The shadow broke clear of the tree cover and fell, black as death, on the silver-white sand. From the pool side the Driller caught Tink's clanging. He lifted his evil head and saw the bundle of light disappear into the cave.

'Coming to Driller, are we?' he sang. 'Coming for the dear twins?' The drill spun happily at his wrist. He loped up the beach and into the cave.

'Damn,' said George Hacker. 'He's gone back into the cave.'

He moved the cursor very slowly up the beach, along the line of boulders, ready now for the familiar black-out before the screen drew the tunnel system. He waited for the inevitable explosion of light that told him that he had been drilled, but nothing came.

'That's funny,' he said.

He nudged further. Still no attack.

'He's gone further in. I wonder why.'

He moved the cursor deeper than ever into the maze, following the Driller's trail.

'Into the stream first,' said Wendy.

'What?' Colin gaped in amazement.

'You're all filthy,' she repeated. 'When was the last time you had a bath?'

'A bath?' asked Hardly.

'Well, a wash, then,' suggested Wendy, thinking this might be easier to remember.

The Lost Boys looked at each other doubtfully.

'Don't need baths,' said Hardly. 'Not in Neverland.'

'You certainly don't have them,' Wendy agreed. 'But that isn't the same as not needing them.'

'I can't,' said Bins. 'Not in the stream. Not with my ass-mar.'

Wendy sighed. This was going to be more difficult than she thought.

'I don't mind,' said Colin. He gestured to the others. 'They smell, anyhow.'

'What?' Bins squealed.

'You do. You're the worst.'

He turned and left them.

'We don't,' Bins argued. But he looked anxiously at Wendy.

'Oh, dear,' she said. 'He's right, I'm afraid. You do.'

They shuffled off after Colin. He was right in the stream, splashing about, rubbing water over his face, dipping his head right under.

'Is it cold?' Bins asked.

'Yes. Freezing.'

'Can't be,' said Hardly. 'It's sunny.'

'Always cold in a stream. The water's fast.'

Matthew stripped off his pyjamas. Looter stepped in and lifted the little boy down.

'Is it?' asked Bins.

They nodded their heads, teeth chattering. Reluctantly the others stepped in, Bins last.

'What about you?' demanded Matthew.

'I'm not dirty,' said Wendy.

'Are.' Matthew pointed.

'You're covered in dirt,' accused Bins.

He was right. Smears of sticky resin had glued dirt to Wendy's arms and face.

'Not in my clothes,' she said. 'The kaftan would spoil.'

'Take it off,' ordered Matthew. He pointed to his pyjamas. He forgot that they had only recently moved into separate bedrooms.

'I'll go upstream,' agreed Wendy.

She spread her kaftan and then her nightdress on the bank in the warm sun and stepped into the icy water. From the forest the eyes watched her with a worried gaze.

'Will she ever fly back?'

'Perhaps.'

'It's very late for her.'

'Yes.'

'She was too old to come, really.'

'Perhaps.'

Downstream, the boys were squealing and growling with delight. Even Bins had forgotten his asthma and was cavorting in the clear shallow water. When Wendy returned, warm in her dry clothes, they were pink, clean and glowing with pleasure.

'Come on. Time to eat,' she called. They waded out, dragging heavy legs through the water.

'You'll soon dry,' she encouraged them. 'Bank up the fire. We'll have some more fish. But don't get dirty again.'

After tea they were warm, clean and satisfied. Wendy looked at them with a pleased air.

'You're much better,' she said. 'You look a nice lot.'

Bins smirked and drew closer to her. This time she squeezed his hand gladly.

'Did I really smell?'

'A little,' she admitted. When his face fell she added, 'But not as much as some of the others. And not at all now.' He was comforted and beamed roundly at her.

'That's the best food I've ever had here,' he said.

This reminded Wendy. 'Where does the other come from?' she asked. 'The junk?'

'At the end of the beach,' Hardly explained.

'By where all the noise comes from,' Colin said.

James nodded. 'You remember. The clanging and booming.'

'What is it?' Wendy wondered.

'Dunno,' said Bins. 'Never go any further. Just take the food from the bins and come back.'

'Sounds like building,' Colin said.

'Oh, well,' Wendy gave up.

They took some trout to Peter but he did not move.

'Will he get better?' asked Matthew.

'I don't know.'

'Tink would know,' said Looter.

'Tink? Where is Tink? What's happened to her?' asked Wendy. She had forgotten her all day.

'Oh, she comes and goes,' said Bins.

'No she doesn't,' said Looter.

''S right,' agreed Colin. 'Not when Peter's here she doesn't.'

'She's always with Peter,' Hardly confirmed.

'Not now,' commented James.

'Well,' said Wendy, brightly, 'I think we can worry about that in the morning. Time for bed.'

'What about the twins?' asked James. 'We can't leave them. Peter wouldn't want us to.'

'In the morning,' Wendy decided. 'It's been a good day. We've got a new place to live, a new house, good food, and we're clean as well. And in the morning we can start to get Peter better. A good sleep will do him a world of good.' Mrs Hacker was a great believer in a good sleep, and the Lost Boys seemed to remember that they had once had mothers who said things like that, so they were quick to agree. Only James wanted to argue. The others were so tired with their work and their bath and so pleased to have Wendy taking charge that they were happy to do anything she said.

They lay quietly together in the pine shelter. Matthew, as always, was close to Looter. Colin, alone, half wished he had a cigarette to finish the day with, but he wasn't sure. Hardly fell asleep instantly, his forehead crinkled with a worried frown. Bins shyly put his hand into Wendy's.

'Thank you,' he whispered.

She smiled down at him in the dusk and they all slept.


The bedouin tents huddled tight to the ground under the palm trees. An orange glow broke from a cooking pit when the coals split and fell, opening bright scars against the grey dust. The three royal children dipped greasy fingers into bowls of fragrant water. They raised fine linen to their lips and brushed away scraps of lamb and beads of sweet fat. Ali rose, bowed to the servants to dismiss them and led his sisters to their tent. When the flap closed

behind the children, the servants dragged the rest of the lamb's carcass from the charcoal pit and ripped away the flesh and filled their own bellies. Their contented chattering comforted the prince and princesses in their ornate comfort of rugs and cushions.

'What happened next?' asked Ali.

'Don't let it be frightening,' begged Amina.

Rahila smoothed her long glossy hair in a black stripe down her back.

'I'm afraid it is, rather,' she warned her little sister.

'Good,' breathed Ali.

'Oh, dear,' Amina wailed. 'It will be all right, won't it?'

Rahila crinkled her brow in thought. 'I don't know.'

'Go on,' urged Ali.

Rahila began.

'Squat, ugly shapes loped through the dark spaces of the forest. Heavy axes glistened in the moonlight. In their shelter the children slept, believing themselves to be safely hidden.'

'Oh no,' Amina whimpered.

'Hush,' Ali ordered her.

'We'll go back to their house,' the Driller explained.

'What about them?' Slee pointed to the children.

'They can stay here. They don't know anything now.'

'Eat them,' urged Loder.

The other trolls looked hopefully at the Driller.

'Hungry,' agreed Cheko. 'Need good food to go hunting.'

The Driller hesitated. He supposed he couldn't keep the twins there for ever without letting the trolls eat them. Samneric saw the indecision in his face and quaked. The trolls noticed it too and grew excited.

'Eat now,' grunted Jooks. He lifted his axe and waved it over his head like a butcher with a meat cleaver.

Strakey chuckled. 'Sweet boys.' He ran a floppy tongue over thick lips.

'No,' decided the Driller. 'Get them all together first. One each, or you'll fall out.'

Slee sniffed. 'All right,' he agreed. 'But eat them anyway if we don't get the other boys tonight.'

'You'll eat them when I say so,' snapped the Driller. 'I got them.'

The trolls shuffled. Jooks tested the edge of his axe with his thumb. Despite its huge bulk it was razor-sharp.

'Our cave,' he said, sulkily. 'Eat what we like.'

'Now look here,' the Driller began. But before he could go any further he was interrupted by a silent movement to his left shutting out some of the glow from the fire pit. There was a sudden jangling.

'Tink,' whispered Sam. 'Peter's here.' They hugged one another with joy and got ready to join in the fight. The trolls growled angrily and the drill whined into life.

'Ready boys,' the Driller ordered. 'Axes high!' He swept his eyes round the cavern. 'Where are you?' he demanded. 'Speak up.'

'He can't,' Tink jangled.

'What?'

'He doesn't speak.'

'Who?'

'Peter.'

'Come on,' the Driller challenged him.

The shadow rose up from the floor and stood, upright at last.

'What's that?' whispered Eric.

'Peter.'

'No. He's not there.'

'Look,' jangled Tink. 'It's Peter. The real Peter. He wants to help you.'

The Driller laughed.

'It's only a shadow.'

'Only a shadow now. But if you get rid of the other Peter then he'll be free. And we'll be on your side.'

'Get rid of the other one?' hissed the Driller.

'Yes.'

'Where is he?'

'We'll show you.'

'Now?'

'Come on.' Tink darted away. The shadow beckoned.

'Come on, boys.'

Samneric watched them disappear into the gloom.

'What can we do?'

'Follow them. Escape.'

'Too late. They've gone. We'll get lost.'

They looked into the gloom, eyes baffled by the darkness. Deep in the tunnels their nightmare waited.

George Hacker sat in his dressing gown, ready for bed. He moved the cursor along the beach but the Driller was nowhere to be found. He tried the pool. Nothing. The cave entrance was empty. The boulders hid nothing. Probing into the jungle at the western edge of the beach he met with no answering threat.

'What's he up to?' he wondered.

'Come to bed.'

'Soon.'

His eye was suddenly drawn to the cave. The Driller appeared, hesitated, then moved quickly away. The ugly little shapes that Mr Hacker had seen before in the tunnels led into the jungle away from him. There was a darker patch and a confusion of sparkling. The Driller moved after them. 'What are they up to?' he repeated. 'Are they running away from me?' He followed cautiously. 'Or are they on the hunt?'

Squat, ugly shapes loped through the dark spaces of the forest. Heavy axes glistened in the moonlight. In their shelter the children slept, believing themselves to be safely hidden. Peter's shadow, always upright now, led the trolls ever nearer. Tink danced and clanged encouragement. The Driller smiled.

# Ten

MRS Hacker sat bolt upright in bed and screamed.

'I'll get you a drink,' said her husband.

He brought up two glasses of weak whiskey and water. They sat up in bed and sipped them together.

'The eyes?' he asked.

'No. Not this time.'

'What?'

'I don't know.'

'Try.'

'Ugly, twisted figures. With cruel faces. Hunting.'

'Yes.'

'Dwarves?'

'Something like that.'

He took her empty glass.

'Try to sleep. It's nothing.'

'No.'

'Good night.'

He lay in silence and listened to hear her breathing tell him that she had gone back to sleep. He stared into the darkness, remembering the line of squat hunters he had tracked into the jungle.

Colin was also dreaming. He was back in the little house

he had searched for the day he got lost. There was a fire burning in the grate. He could smell fresh toast. Outside, huge white flakes of snow floated from a black sky, but he was warm and happy. He lifted a piece of toast to his lips. A voice shouted, 'No! Don't. Don't!' Colin was puzzled. Why should he not eat toast? It screamed louder. 'Don't! Please!' Thick arms wrapped themselves round him. The toast smell changed to a disgusting stink of sweat and foul breath. Colin gagged. He opened his eyes and looked straight into Slee's ugly face. Troll eyes were screwed up with greedy delight. Spit dribbled out of his hungry mouth.

'Don't! Don't!' Hardly was yelling, his little thin body twisting frantically. Jooks held him tight in his arms.

'Fat one,' gurgled Strakey, lugging Bins towards the forest. 'I got a fat one.'

The pine branches were scattered all over. Peter's shadow had led the trolls and the Driller without hesitation to the pine-fragrant clearing. They pounced on the little house and tore it to pieces. Jooks grabbed Hardly straight away. He was eager to get a boy to eat and trolls are not very clever, so he did not look first. His big, disappointed hands closed on the thin arms. Slee secured Colin before Hardly's shouts of terror had properly woken him up. Strakey was overjoyed to feel how plump and appetising Bins was.

The Driller hung back from the first attack. He wanted Peter.

'Get them,' he ordered Cheko, pointing to the Hackers. Cheko took Matthew in one hand and Wendy in the other, dragging them away roughly.

Peter lay still as death through all this. He was curled around James's staff. This central support of the pine-branch house had not moved under the trolls' ferocious attack. James, one hand on the staff for balance, was shaking Peter with his other hand.

'Wake up. Help! Peter! Help!'

Peter lay still.

The Driller surveyed the scene. All the children were captured. The trolls went shuffling off back to their caves with their trophies. Tink darted around the clearing, jangling and clanking her amusement. Peter's shadow lurked at the edge, waiting. James and Peter, one in an injured sleep, the other helpless and unarmed, crouched before the Driller. The drill whined eagerly. Lips parted over steel teeth in a final grin of victory. Peter was his. First to get rid of the other brat.

'Out of the way,' he ordered. He grabbed James to fling him aside.

The trolls reeled back in pain. A brilliant light, cold as ice, sharp as a two-edged sword, sliced through the night. The Driller fell back from James with an injured bellow.

The trolls dropped their heads, sniffed fearfully and in blind panic shambled back into the forest towards their cave. Cheko, who was nearest the light and had been most hurt by it, stood amazed, Wendy in one hand and Matthew struggling in the other. He dropped Matthew and unslung his axe from where it hung on the broad leather strap across his back. Wendy watched, frozen in disbelief, as he raised its ugly double head to hack her little brother to pieces.

'James!' she shouted. 'Peter!'

James was hanging bewildered to his staff. Peter did not move. The axe hung poised over Matthew's head, ready to fall.

A tall, slim body stepped from the trees and snatched away the axe. As Cheko turned in further astonishment to see what had happened, a bright blade flashed through the moonlight, taking off his head. He slumped gracelessly to the needle-strewn floor. On either side of where he had stood were the slim creatures who had disarmed and killed him. Their large bright eyes flashed the moon to Wendy. Each held a slender sword, and one still held Cheko's axe.

'Oh no!' she wailed.

'Wait,' ordered the one with the axe. Wendy dipped down, scooped Matthew into her arms and lifted both him and herself from the clearing.

'Stop!' the figures shouted.

Wendy soared higher, flew over the trees and towards the moon. She was shaking so dreadfully that she nearly lost her grip on Matthew.

'Oh,' she complained.

'It's all right. Let go.'

'What?'

'I can fly, too. Let go.'

Gratefully, Wendy loosened her grip on Matthew. He flew more steadily than she.

'I'm falling,' Wendy complained.

'Try.'

'It's no good.' She reached out a hand and he steadied her. Together they drifted back down to the ground. The forest had ended and they came to rest at the edge of the lake.

'What's wrong?'

'I can't fly any more. It's gone.'

Matthew leaped into the air. 'I can. Try.'

'It's no good.'

They sat together at the lakeside, cuddling for comfort, and watched the sun dye the water at dawn.

'He was horrible, wasn't he?' said Matthew.

'Yes.'

'That axe.'

'Don't think about it.'

'No. What will we do?'

'I don't know.'

While Cheko was losing his head, Peter's shadow stole over to the Driller and beckoned him into the forest. The Driller was very shaken by the blast that had sent him spinning across the clearing. His moustache was singed and the drill was screaming, and there was a ringing in his ears like an alarm clock, but he followed the shadow into the trees.

The forest grew silent after the skirmish. The trolls were already back in their tunnels, dragging the terrified Lost Boys through the maze to the fire cavern.

'Oh,' said the slender figure with Cheko's axe. 'What a mess.'

'Yes.'

'We've lost them all.'

They looked at the deserted clearing. Driller, Lost Boys, Wendy, Matthew, Tink, Shadow. All gone.

'Yes.'

'Except for them.'

'Yes, we've got them.'

They stepped towards the ruins of the little house. Their swords glinted. The broad, double-headed axe swung carelessly. James crouched by Peter and raised his head to look up at them.

The trolls were tired and frightened when they reached the fire cavern.

'Eat,' growled Strakey.

Bins squeaked in terror.

'What about Driller?' asked Slee nervously.

'Driller's dead,' said Strakey. 'Saw him.'

'Driller doesn't die that easy.'

'Eat,' repeated Strakey.

'We'll wait,' Slee insisted. He looked to the others for support.

Jooks felt Hardly's thin arm in his hand. He saw how plump Bins was. Perhaps they would get mixed up if they waited. He liked the look of the fat one.

'Tomorrow,' he agreed. 'Sleep first.'

They flung their boys into a heap by Samneric and sloped off to get to sleep.

'Oooh,' wailed Bins.

'Shut up,' snapped Colin.

'Where's Peter?' asked the twins.

The Lost Boys fell into silence.

'Well?'

'He's ill.'

'Might be dead.'

'Don't know.'

Samneric screwed up their faces.

'He'll be all right,' said Looter. 'You'll see.'

'He'll come for us?' insisted Eric, or it might have been Sam.

'No,' Colin argued. 'He's probably dead. He's ill anyway. Can't wake up. We'll have to get out on our own. Which way?'

The twins explained about the nightmares in the tunnels.

'Got to do something,' Colin decided. 'I'm trying.'

He stretched out his arms in front of him and felt his way from the glow of the fire pit to the edge of the cavern, taking care not to follow the way the trolls had gone to the corners where they slept. At last his fingers found the wall. In front, all was black. Behind, he could see the outlines of the Lost Boys crouched in the fire's glow. They had not moved to follow him.

He fingered his way fearfully round the rough wall, searching for the first tunnel to lead away from the huge cavern. Soon the stone turned away from the fire and into deeper blackness. He drew in his breath and stepped into the tunnel, arms outstretched. A long, bony hand met his fingers and grabbed at him. He snatched his hand away, turned and fled back to the light of the fire and the company of the Lost Boys.

'What was it?' breathed Hardly.

Colin shook his head.

'We'd better sleep,' advised Looter.

The boys settled themselves close together for comfort and fell asleep. Except for Colin. He did not think he could ever close his eyes again. He stared into the darkness in the direction of the tunnel he had strayed into. His eyes ached with the strain of keeping them open but he was determined not to sleep while he was in the caves, perhaps never to sleep again. Slowly his eyelids lowered and he slept sitting up.

Peter's shadow helped the Driller to get clear of the pine glade. He led him through the forest, Tink jangling somewhere near.

'No further,' insisted the Driller. 'Enough.'

He sank to the ground. His hand stung from where he had grabbed the staff to hit at James. His head still rang. His eyes could not get a clear focus.

'All right in the morning,' he said. 'Rest.' He slept fitfully, disturbed by the nearby lapping of the waves on the lakeside.


'Leave him alone!' James shouted. 'I'll smash you. Like I did him.' He pointed to where the Driller had fallen but the place was already empty.

The two slender figures fell back.

'More.' James snatched the dagger from Peter's belt and brandished it at them. Their large oval eyes stared back at him.

'We can help,' said the one with the axe.

'I saw you. You killed him,' James shouted.

'Yes.'

'Well, get out.'

'It was a troll.'

'He was going to kill the boy,' agreed the other.

James lowered the dagger.

'Where are they?' he demanded.

'Dragged off by the trolls.'

'All of them?' James had lost sight of much of the struggle.

'Not the girl.'

'Nor the little boy.'

'They flew off.'

James gave a grim smile. He hoisted himself to his feet, holding the staff for support.

'Who are you?'

'Edoril,' said the one with the axe.

'Galadrey.'

They were several inches taller than James when he stood to face them, but looked no older. Dawn threw light on their faces.

'We can help,' repeated Edoril. He dropped the axe, turned and left the glade.

Galadrey sheathed his sword and smiled. 'You beat the Driller,' he said.

'Is he dead? Did I kill him?'

'No. But it was a powerful spell.'

James was puzzled. 'I don't know what happened. He grabbed me and I shook him off. Then there was this blinding light. The next thing I knew he was on the other side of the clearing and your . . .'

'Edoril.'

'Edoril was killing the troll.'

'Were you holding your wand?'

James looked at the staff. 'This?'

'Yes.'

'I suppose so.'

'Come on,' said Galadrey. He stepped forward with empty hands upturned. 'Be friends, James.'

'How do you know my name?' James demanded, all suspicion again.

'We have watched you. Ever since you came to our forest.'

'Spying.'

'If we had not, the girl would be with the trolls and the little boy dead.'

James considered this. Edoril returned, hands full of herbs. He stooped by the embers of their fire and blew them to life. Taking some water from a flask he infused the herbs in a small bowl over the embers.

'You have to trust us,' said Galadrey.

'Why?'

Edoril smiled. 'Because you have no one else.' He swirled the infusion in his bowl. Steam rose. 'Come.' He approached James. 'Lift Peter's head.'

James did not move.

'Please,' said Galadrey. 'There is not much time.'

'You do it,' said James.

'I cannot.'

'Why?'

'You were holding the wand. You must lift him. I can help if you start.'

James slid his hand under Peter's head. Galadrey helped. Edoril put the bowl to his lips and tilted it. Water, green-stained and aromatic, trickled down Peter's chin.

'Move his lips,' Edoril instructed James.

The infusion went into his mouth. Some of it spilled out but Peter's throat gulped the rest down.

'Enough,' decided Edoril.

They laid his head back on the ground.

'Tell him to get up.'

'What?'

'Stand. Hold your wand. Tell him to get up.'

James did as he was told. He looked more sturdy and powerful than ever in contrast with the two slender friends. His robe added to his impressive appearance.

'Get up,' he ordered Peter.

Nothing happened. James blushed.

'This is silly,' he protested.

'You don't mean it,' said Galadrey.

'You want to get rid of the Driller, don't you?' asked Edoril.

'Yes.'

'And you wanted to get rid of Peter,' added Galadrey.

'No.'

'You did. When you flung him away you wanted to be rid of him, didn't you?'

James looked away.

'You need him back now,' Galadrey continued. 'If you want to rescue the others.'

'Can we?' asked James. 'Wendy and Matthew. Can we really get them back?'

'We might,' said Edoril. '*You* might. If you make Peter better.'

'And the Lost Boys,' said Galadrey. 'Them first.'

James looked down at Peter. 'Get up, please,' he begged.

Peter did not move.

'You must not ask,' said Edoril.

'Tell him,' said Galadrey.

'Get up. Now. You're better. Get up.'

The chatter of birds in the glade stopped suddenly. The breeze dropped. Somewhere in the forest a fox yelped out a barking cough. All fell silent.

'Get up.' James's voice slipped from its usual high pitch and boomed out the words.

Peter rolled over on to his side. Galadrey reached down a hand and took his arm. Peter stumbled up to his knees.

Edoril held out the bowl. 'Drink.'

Peter drained it, leaving the soggy leaves in the bottom. Slowly his face cleared and he looked at the three of them. His eyes met James's, then turned away. He examined the other two.

'You,' he said.

They smiled.

'Do you know them?' asked James.

'No.'

'Then?'

'We keep to ourselves,' said Galadrey.

'And we work,' said Edoril. 'Peter likes to play.'

'They made you better,' said James.

'You made him better,' Galadrey corrected him.

'Him?' said Peter.

'Of course. You knew he could.'

Peter shrugged.

'Did you not tell him anything?'

'Tell me what?' James asked.

'Peter went to fetch you,' Edoril explained, 'but I don't think he meant it. He didn't want to. Peter likes to do things himself.'

'I brought him, didn't I?' Peter objected.

'Yes. But you didn't tell him. So things are worse than before.'

'The trolls have got the Lost Boys,' Galadrey told him. 'And the Driller is on the trail of the others.' He paused. 'Wendy and Matthew.'

'That's right,' said James, 'but is he? I thought he'd gone.'

'He has. But he's gone after them, I fear. With your shadow,' he said to Peter. 'And that nasty little friend of yours.'

'So there's a lot to do,' Galadrey suggested.

'Wendy,' said James. 'We'll go after her.'

Edoril shook his head.

'First,' he said, 'you'll both rest, and eat. Night is the most dangerous time. And you must rescue the Lost Boys first. They are already captured and in great danger. Wendy and Matthew are still free.'

'For the moment,' said Galadrey.

'For the moment,' Edoril agreed.

'I still don't understand,' James said. 'What didn't Peter tell me?'

'Well?' asked Galadrey.

Peter stared obstinately at him, then said, 'About the wizard.'

'Wizard?'

'The wizard who will lead the Lost Boys home and save the Neverland.'

'What wizard? Where is he?' James demanded. 'Let's get him to help us.'

Peter and Edoril and Galadrey looked at James. His hands were on his staff, feet firmly apart, his robe fell with severe authority from his shoulders. His head was high and defiant.

'Oh, dear,' said Galadrey. 'You have been very bad, Peter. He still doesn't know.'

'Oh, bother!' Peter stamped his foot. 'You'll spoil everything. You always do. I hate elves.'

'Elves,' said James. 'Are you really elves?'

'We are,' said Galadrey quietly. 'And you are the wizard,'

'Me?'

The pit that the servants had dug to roast the sheep breathed out puffs of grey ash. Cold on top, it still glowed hot deep in its heart.

'Let's move on,' Ali suggested.

'Shall we?' asked Amina. She asked Ali but she looked at Rahila.

'If you like,' Rahila agreed. She turned away and walked past the tents to the lakeside. Amina trotted beside her.

'Finish the story before we go. Please.'

Rahila shook her head. She stared across the lake, screwing up her eyes against the morning brightness.

'What are you looking for?' asked Ali, who had joined them.

'Nothing. I don't know.'

'Please finish the story,' Amina pleaded. 'Tell her to, Ali.'

Ali too was anxious to know what would happen next, but he was too proud to ask his sister.

'Stories are for the darkness,' she said, 'not for the daylight.'

'Tonight, then,' said Ali.

'No.'

'Oh, please,' squealed Amina. 'You can't leave it like that.'

The soft waves mumbled at the pebbles.

'The story's here,' said Rahila. 'There can't be anything to tell if we move on.'

'Then we'll stay. We'll stay, won't we?' demanded Amina.

Ali pursed his lips. The hooded falcon on his arm reared up and spread its wings. Rahila ignored them and kept her face to the lake, her eyes scanning the far bank as though waiting for something, or someone, to appear.

'All right,' agreed Ali. 'One more night. All right?'

'Is it?' Amina asked. 'Is it enough? Will you finish the story tonight?'

Rahila smiled at her little sister. 'Yes,' she said at last. 'I think it will be over tonight.'

Ali, satisfied, walked away.

'And a happy ending. It must have a happy ending.'

'I don't know. We'll see.'

# *Eleven*

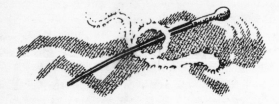

I T was a lonely day.

The silence of the breakfast table pierced through George Hacker. He mooched through the children's rooms, looking for signs, anything that might promise him that they would return. He swept aside James's troll army with an impatient wave of his arm. He flicked the switch of Matthew's computer. He picked up Wendy's new shoes and carried them back to the kitchen.

'These aren't very nice, are they?' he said.

'They're comfortable. They won't hurt her feet.'

'Huh.'

He dropped them to the floor and dragged himself off to work.

It was a sleepy day.

The Driller dozed on and off. At his wrist the drill kept up a never-ending hum of anger and pain. Peter's shadow, upright now, darted in and out of the trees and down to the lake. Tink hovered in a bored and fretful fashion. She changed her earrings several times, put a new stud in her nose, painted her fingernails red and her toenails blue and experimented with some make-up.

'How's that?' she asked Peter's shadow with a leer. Shadows cannot speak even when they have escaped so she jangled off crossly.

It was a smelly day.

Colin toppled over in his sleep and woke with a start. At first he could not make out where he was and he thought the glow from the fire pit was a campfire in the forest. Then the smell hammered into him and he felt a tug of fear at the back of his neck as he remembered the cold, bony hand that had reached out of the darkness at him. He snuggled closer to the other Lost Boys and fell back into a disturbing slumber.

It was a bitter day.

Wendy and Matthew scratched around by the lakeside.

'Try,' he urged. 'Please.'

'It's no good. I can't any more. I just can't fly.'

'But why?'

Wendy thought she knew, but it was no good trying to tell Matthew; he was too little. What was the point of growing up if it stopped you doing the things you liked doing? What was the point if it meant you couldn't explain things any more?

'I just can't.'

'Well, how will we get home if we can't fly?'

'Do you want to?'

'What?'

'Go home. You wanted to come here so much.'

Once Matthew would have fallen to the floor and screamed, kicking his legs about. Not now. But his face went slack and sad.

'It's all right,' said Wendy. 'We'll find a way.'

They slept again, holding each other for comfort after the frightening and wakeful night. It was past noon when they woke again with dry, bad-tasting mouths.

'Let's go to the lake and drink,' said Wendy. 'We'll feel better then.'

It was a magical day.

'You should have told James,' Galadrey rebuked Peter.

'I wasn't sure, was I?'

'Sure?'

They sat round Edoril's fire. Peter was better. He had a lump on the side of his forehead where he had struck the tree, and he still rubbed his side from time to time where the pain was, or had been, but otherwise he had recovered from his headlong flight across the pine glade.

'He might not have been,' he argued. 'It might just have been a stick.'

Edoril smiled.

'And just a dressing gown?' he asked with amusement.

'Yes.'

'Stand up, James.'

James stood and immediately assumed his Neverland posture, feet apart, hands on the staff, head high, robe flowing down. The other three looked at him long and hard until he grew embarrassed and sat down again quickly. Peter looked ashamed.

'Very well,' agreed Galadrey. 'He showed you it wasn't just a stick in the end, anyway.'

'But what?' asked James. 'What can I do?'

'Anything,' said Peter.

'Not quite,' Galadrey corrected him. 'But quite a lot.'

James looked from one to another in mounting excitement.

'But be careful,' warned Edoril. 'It's dangerous.'

'Why?'

'A lot of power always is.'

Peter got up and slouched off. He walked a few paces, then hopped into the air and circled the clearing.

'What can go wrong?' James wanted to know.

'If you use it wrongly it will hurt you.'

'And if you meet one with greater power it will rebound on to you,' warned Galadrey. 'So don't do just anything you want.'

'Or the first thing that comes into your head.'

'Think.'

'And use the least power you need to.'

'And watch whom you use it against.'

This was too much, too fast. James was bewildered.

'Who might I be against?'

'We don't know.'

'Not yet.'

'Not until you get into the tunnels.'

'The tunnels?' James asked in alarm.

'Where the trolls are.'

'To get the Lost Boys.'

'What about Wendy and Matthew?' he demanded.

'Later.'

'Lost Boys first.'

'But I don't even know what I can do. I don't know how to use the power.'

Peter stepped off a branch high above them and drifted contemptuously down.

'He'll mess it up,' he predicted.

'Shut up,' said James, and he lifted his staff.

'See,' said Peter. 'He doesn't think.'

James lowered his arm.

'He might,' said Galadrey and Edoril together.

'Might what?' asked James.

'Might mess it up,' said Edoril.

'Might learn to think,' said Galadrey.

'What do you want?' Edoril asked Peter.

Peter said nothing for a long time. 'I don't know,' he admitted at last. 'I want the Lost Boys back. I want this pain to go away. I want the Neverland.'

'Always?' asked Galadrey.

'I suppose so.'

'And what about you?' Galadrey turned to James.

'I want Wendy and Matthew. I want to help the Lost Boys.' He glared at Peter. 'I want to help him.'

'Do you?' asked Galadrey.

'Yes.'

'Do you really?' asked Peter.

'Yes.'

'And?' Edoril prompted him.

'And I want to go home.'

Peter grinned. 'Home?'

'Yes.'

'And leave me the Neverland?'

'Of course.'

Peter soared up to the branches crowing. His face was red with delight when he spiralled back down.

'Do you really want to go home?'

'Of course.'

'I thought you'd want to stay here always and be a magician, a wizard, and have the power.'

'I don't even know how,' James protested.

Peter grabbed his shoulders. 'We'll show you. Won't we?'

The elves nodded.

James grinned shyly at Peter. 'We'll get the Lost Boys back,' he promised.

'Together,' Peter shouted.

'There are things to do first,' said Galadrey. 'Things for James to learn.'

'Come on,' said Peter. 'Let's get started.'

They smiled at one another.

'No. Rest first,' warned Edoril. 'You've had a long bad night, and an even longer one to come. Sleep. Then, in the afternoon, we will prepare James for the caves.'


The late afternoon sun was laying a golden road across the lake when Matthew found the canoes.

'Look here,' he called to Wendy.

They were moored in an overgrown inlet. The once bright colours had faded but the children could still see the patterns decorating the animal skins stretched over the wooden struts: a bear's claw; a great eagle, wings spread; a buffalo; a charging horse; and, on the best of the craft, an intricate flower.

'What's that?' asked Matthew.

'A tiger lily.'

'Let's try it.'

He pulled the mooring rope from its branch and stepped into the canoe.

'Steady,' warned Wendy. Too late. The boat rolled and Matthew was pitched into the water. He came up spluttering.

'It's all right. It isn't deep.'

He was right. The water only reached his waist. He waded towards the open lake, towing the canoe. Wendy stopped and picked up the little paddles that had floated off after the accident. Once clear of the trees they both climbed in.

'This is fun.'

'Careful.'

'Let's go. Right out on the lake. As far as we can.'

'No, it's dangerous. Just a little way, then we'll turn back.'

The canoe handled easily under their paddles and they were soon far from the shore.

'Turn back, now.'

They paddled quickly, turning the boat, but a wind picked up, blowing them away from the shore.

'It's no good,' said Matthew. 'We're going backwards.'

'Try.'

They paddled harder. Waves broke over the prow and spilled into the canoe.

'No good.'

They stopped. The canoe was carried by the wind, further from the shore.

'We can't go,' said Wendy, desperately. 'We've got to get back to James and Peter.' She knew it was no good as soon as she said it. Matthew hopped up, left the canoe and grabbed the rope. He flew forwards towards the shore, tugging as hard as he could. Wendy paddled. They moved a little way in the right direction. The waves grew higher and drenched her kaftan.

'Stop,' she shouted. 'We're shipping too much water. We'll sink.'

Matthew dropped the rope and landed back in the canoe. They baled out with cupped hands. All the time the small craft drifted steadily away from land. The two children turned to see where they were going. The boat was in the centre of the line of gold thrown by the sun over the lake.

'Along a golden road,' said Wendy. 'But where to?'

Galadrey, Edoril, Peter and James stood at the mouth of the cave. The trees cast long shadows along the beach in the evening sun. A small disturbance in the golden water of the cove told Peter that the crocodile was making its lonely circle of the wrecked ship.

'Goodbye,' said Galadrey.

'Please come,' begged James.

'No,' said Edoril. 'We cannot.'

'You will win,' Galadrey assured him.

'Come on,' Peter urged. 'Let's go.' His face was set and hard, though he tried to wear a confident smile.

Edoril placed his hand on Peter's shoulder. 'Go well,' he said.

Peter nodded.

The elves strode away into the jungle.

'We must be quick,' said Peter. 'It will be dark soon.'

'Dark enough already, in there.'

'Let's go.' Peter walked out of the light.

James followed. 'It stinks.'

'Shhh.'

'I can't see a thing.'

'Feel your way along the wall,' Peter suggested.

'Uggh. Slime.'

'Keep going.'

James felt his throat growing tight with fear and disgust. The dark, the smell, the slime, the oppressive enclosure of the tunnel, and the trailing spider webs brushing his face were too much for him. He raised his staff to clear a way through the cobwebs. As it rose above the level of his shoulders it glowed faintly, then it burst into a penetrating light. There was a shriek and a scuffling.

'Did you see that?' Peter asked.

'What?'

'The thing that ran away when you lit the tunnel.'

'No. What was it?'

'Don't ask.'

They made their way forward, encouraged by the light. The tunnel turned to the left and forked in two.

'Which way?' asked James.

'Wait,' said Peter.

The staff moved like a compass needle, dragging James's arm with it, pointing to the left.

'On we go,' Peter announced.

Through the maze, always following the staff's directions, the boys drew ever nearer to the trolls' cavern. Sometimes they caught a glimpse of angry eyes blinking at them from a side turning, kept away by the light from the wand. Sometimes a chatter of evil teeth or the menacing scuffling of sharp claws against the rock. But the wand kept away the nightmares that roamed the passageways.

'How much farther?'

Peter shrugged.

'We must be very deep underground.'

The Driller stretched, yawned, clambered to his feet and looked around. There was a bell clanging inside his head. He shook himself and slapped a hand to his forehead. The bell persisted. He stamped his feet. Still it rang. He fired his drill at top speed and bored an angry hole in a tree trunk.

'Oh, don't be so stupid,' the bell clanged at him.

'What?'

'Quickly.' Tink darted in front of him. 'Follow them.'

'Who?'

'Come on.'

He stepped after her and tumbled over, hanging by his right arm from the tree. The drill was buried deep. He snarled, baring his steel teeth, made the drill scream with speed and drew it out. Peter's shadow was hopping impatiently beside him.

'Quick,' Tink urged.

The Driller followed the dark blot and the bundle of sparks. They led him to a canoe moored in the inlet.

'Into the lake,' Tink ordered. 'You'll lose them.'

In moments the Driller was paddling along in the canoe. Tink flew in front of him. The shadow lay on the surface of the water, rippling with the waves.

'See?' Tink asked.

Ahead on the lake, following a golden road of sunlight, were Wendy and Matthew. They looked away from the Driller, towards the other shore.

'She can't fly any more,' Tink told him. 'And he's very little. They're yours.'

'Mine,' he snarled. 'Was it her brother who did this to me?'

'That's right.'

'Onward! On!'

His fierce paddling, assisted by the strong wind, drew him ever closer to the small boat ahead.

# Twelve

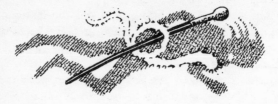

HARDLY moaned in his sleep.

'Mummmm.'

He reached out a hand for Wendy.

'Mum.'

He could not remember his own mother, but Wendy had reminded him of what a mother was and he was crying out for her. He woke Looter.

'Mum.'

'All right.'

Hardly opened his eyes.

'Where are we?'

'In trouble,' said Colin, awake immediately.

'I'm hungry,' Bins complained.

There was a horrid giggle, and a grunt. 'So am I,' said Jooks.

'Oh, dear,' moaned Sam, or it might have been Eric. All the Lost Boys clung to one another. They looked at the row of trolls.

'Now then,' said Slee. 'How many? One, two, three, four, five, six.'

Strakey scratched his head with the handle of his axe.

'What's up?' demanded Slee.

'Is that one each?' Strakey asked.

'Well,' said Jooks. 'Six boys, and . . .'

'One, two, three, four,' counted Loder. 'Four of us.'

'Six is more than four,' said Slee. 'So there isn't enough for one each. You'll have to share.'

'I'm not sharing,' said Strakey. 'I got the fat one.' He pointed to Bins. 'And I'm eating him.' He lurched towards the terrified boy.

'Oohhh,' wailed Bins.

Four axes gleamed in the firelight as four trolls lunged forward, each one anxious not to lose a boy to eat. Strakey closed a thick fist over a plump arm.

'Ooohhhh! Help!' Bins wailed, even louder.

There was a huge clap, like an explosion, and a cold light drenched the cavern. The trolls squealed in pain. Slee dropped his axe and dragged himself to the nearest dark tunnel. Loder covered his eyes with his strange back-to-front hands. Strakey lifted one arm to shield his eyes, still clutching greedily at Bins with his other hand. Jooks lifted his head and howled in pain as the light drilled into his troll's eyes.

Colin took in the confusion quickly. He grabbed Slee's dropped axe and with a mighty heave he swung it over his head to threaten the trolls. The weight was too much for him and instead of hanging in menace it swung right round in his helpless arms and fell back, lopping off the top of Strakey's head in its descent. It slipped out of Colin's hand and clattered to the stone floor. For a second Strakey looked unhurt by the blow and he turned his face in anger towards Colin. Then he slowly closed his eyes, let Bins slip from his grasp and fell, dead.

James remained at the cavern entrance, wand held high, keeping the light as bright as he could. Peter sprang into the air and flew towards the trolls. He plunged his dagger into Jooks's neck. Loder, bewildered by the noise and the terrible light, ran blindly away before Peter could touch him. Peter's dagger was quite small to use against the thick neck of a troll and he took several stabs before Jooks was finished off.

The fierce intensity of the light dimmed to a gentle glow. James walked to the centre of the cave, staff still aloft, his face drawn with pain and effort.

'All right,' said Peter. He put his arm around James's shoulders and led him to the others.

George Hacker slammed his fist on the desk in Matthew's room and swore. The light was fading outside. He could smell his dinner cooking downstairs.

'It's broken,' he complained. 'Must be.'

He had taken his cursor everywhere he could, on the beach, into the cave entrance, through the jungle, but he could not find anyone to fire at. The Driller had disappeared. In desperation he went back to the cave and into the tunnels. Slowly, and with growing anger, he explored the maze of dead ends and blind alleys, impatiently pressing on further and deeper down. He knew that it was desperately important that he should finish the game. If he did not kill the Driller this time then he would never see James and Wendy and Matthew again.

'No, that's stupid,' he mumbled to himself. 'Doesn't make any difference to them whether I get the Driller or not.' But, all the same, he pressed on deeper and deeper into the caves, firing the button over and over at the strange shapes that leaped out at him. They were getting quicker and quicker, more and more cunning all the time.

The Driller paddled tirelessly towards Wendy and Matthew, driven on by his anger. He saw them touch shore, drag their canoe up the beach and above the water mark. They did not turn to look back over the lake but headed along the shore.

The shadow was the first ashore, sliding off the surface of the water and springing upright on the pebbles. The Driller pushed his canoe back into the water and watched it drift away. He strode to the beached craft with the tiger lily painted on its side. In a frenzy he attacked it with his drill, boring ragged holes through it over and over. It would never float again.

'Come on,' Tink jangled. 'Never mind that.'

'Are we all here?' he asked. Peter's shadow was almost invisible as the darkness thickened.

'All here,' Tink assured him.

'Then we go to the girl,' he triumphed.

Samneric were so happy they cried. Bins kept rubbing his arm where Strakey had held him, but there was no harm done. Colin tried not to look too pleased with himself for rescuing Bins. Hardly kept banging Peter on the back. Looter looked down at Loder's body, his face troubled by something, his eyes sad.

'Didn't want to kill them,' he said.

'Only way,' said Colin. 'They were going to eat us.'

'I know. Just doesn't seem right, though.'

'Look at his hands,' said Bins. 'They're like yours.'

Looter plunged his own hands into his pockets, pulled a face, more of surprise than anger, then slowly took one of his hands out. He looked at it. He took out the other and held them side by side. They were the right way round.

'How did you do that?' asked Hardly.

'Didn't do anything.'

'Then what?'

'Don't know.'

'Doesn't matter,' said Peter. 'All sorts of things happen when there's a wizard about, don't they, James?'

James gripped his wand. 'We've got to go,' he said. 'There's Wendy and Matthew to see to.'

Peter agreed. 'We came in this way,' he said.

They formed up and got ready to leave the cave. Colin wanted to bring the axe with him but it was too heavy to carry. They stepped into the tunnel and instantly the light faded from the wand and they were in utter darkness. They scuttled back to the cavern and the staff glowed again. They tried again. Again the light faded.

'What's wrong?' Peter asked James.

'I don't understand it. I'm doing everything I can. It just goes out.'

'Try again.'

No better. James walked to the centre of the cave, held the wand high. It glowed brightly. He kept it in the air until slowly it lowered itself and pointed to a different tunnel, nearly opposite to the one through which they had entered.

'This way,' said James. They all followed. In this tunnel the wand kept alight.

'But where are we going?' asked Peter.

'Dunno. Quick way out?'

'Not going out,' said Colin.

'No?'

'Going further in. Look.'

He was right. The way sloped down with every step they took. They were heading deeper and deeper.

'Why?' asked Bins.

'Got no choice,' said James. 'We go in darkness or we let the wand lead us. No choice.'

'What for?'

'Must be something else to do down here. Something else to fight?'

They all remembered their own nightmares hiding in the tunnels. The way sloped down. Water began to trickle down the rough stone walls.

'What about Wendy?' Bins asked.

'Can't help,' James regretted. 'Can't do anything without the wand. And it's taking us this way.'

Wendy and Matthew were tired again when they had beached the canoe. Matthew slumped to the ground and hugged himself. He suddenly looked very small in his pyjamas. Wendy laid her hand on his head and ruffled his hair.

'Come on.'

'Where?'

'There's nothing here.'

'Tired. Want to go to sleep.'

'Not far, I think.' She tugged his arm.

Matthew threw himself out on the pebbles and twisted his face. His mouth opened to scream but nothing came out. Slowly he closed it again. He looked up at Wendy. 'Do we have to?' he asked politely.

'I think so. I don't like the feel of it here. And besides, look, there's a palm tree over there. See?' Matthew screwed up his eyes in the failing light. 'There might be some dates, or a coconut. Perhaps some grass to lie in. Come on. It isn't far.'

Matthew nodded. He stood up, left his tantrum on the beach for ever, and walked through the subsiding pebbles hand in hand with Wendy. Two, three, more palm trees came into view, then the pointed tents.

'Hurrah,' gloated Matthew. 'People. There'll be food, and somewhere to sleep.'

'Yes,' Wendy agreed cautiously. 'People.'

The cursor flashed every time it hit a dead end in the tunnels, and a siren wailed. George swore. He kept his thumb on the 'fire' button. The path behind him was littered with the corpses of mutilated mutations he had killed on his journey. The indicator registered that he had scored over 73,000 points. He was tired, and his back ached. His hands were stiff from manipulating the controls, but fear for the children drove him on. He turned from the false path he had just taken and retraced his steps. At the next corner an angular shape hurtled towards him. He stabbed the button and the machine squealed. The counter added another 1,000 points to his score. He pressed on.

'It's no good,' Rahila protested. 'I can't.' She sipped her mint tea distractedly and smoothed an anxious hand over her black hair.

'Why not?'

'You must.'

'Please.' Amina begged.

'What will happen to them?' Ali demanded.

Rahila spread her hands out in a gesture of helplessness. 'I don't know.'

'Make up some more.' Ali ordered. 'Go on.'

'Don't you see?' Rahila said. 'I don't know what happens next. It's too frightening to think.'

'Pooh,' scoffed her brother. 'Too frightening. When you have me with you?' He leaped to his feet and drew his scimitar.

'Another one,' Colin called out.

The boys slowed down. In the path in front of them the wand threw its light on to the corpse of a nightmare. It was thin and tiny, a body no bigger than a baby, but with a huge head and with two legs and four arms that broke from its body in long angles.

'Ugggh,' said Bins.

'Like a daddy-long-legs,' said Looter.

'Whose is it?' Peter asked them.

'Mine,' admitted Hardly.

'Often?' asked James.

'Quite a lot. Not every night. Only sometimes.'

'Well. I think it's gone now,' James reassured him.

Hardly nodded, but his face was white with loathing.

'All right,' said Peter, 'On we go.'

No one liked to kick it or touch it in any way, so they stepped over the body of the nightmare and carried on. James's arms ached from holding the staff high. He was troubled by the dead monsters on the path.

'Why?' he asked Peter. 'Why are they all dead?'

'Don't know. Good job though.' He grinned.

James clicked his tongue.

'You've done it,' Colin suggested. 'With the wand. It gets them when we come near.'

James shook his head. 'I'd know if it was that. I'd feel it.'

'Perhaps the caves are dying?' Peter offered.

'Maybe.'

'Can't we stop?' Bins begged.

'Must get on,' said James.

'I hate these tunnels. They're horrible.'

It was true. They were vile. The boys no longer noticed the stink, but the walls were slimy, the floor sharp and uneven. Sometimes the roof dropped low so that they had to walk with their backs bent, arms dangling like trolls. This was the worst time for James and the most difficult to keep the wand aloft.

Perhaps we'll turn into trolls, he thought in panic when his back was bent under the low rock. Perhaps the trolls were Lost Boys who came for shelter into the cave and couldn't get out.

The water no longer ran down the walls and it seemed to Peter that the slope of the floor had turned and now began to lead them up, but his legs were so tired that he couldn't be sure.

'I don't know,' Colin said again. 'Looks like someone's been here already and killed them off.'

'Who?' Peter asked.

'Doesn't matter,' said Looter. 'As long as they're dead.'

'What if it's the Driller, though? What if we turn the next corner and he's there?'

'What if it's not the Driller?' James warned.

They moved on, fearfully.

# *Thirteen*

T HE horses flared their nostrils and whimpered in alarm. The camels, dense and unconcerned, regurgitated cud, chewed it again and blinked at the rising moon. The noise of the horses carried through the sharp cold of the night air of the desert, beyond Matthew and Wendy, reaching the Driller's ears. In agitation he wiped the sweat from his head on the arm of his striped shirt. He parted his lips beneath the red moustache, half in a greedy smile, half in joyful expectation of the struggle soon to come. The drill whirred.

'George!'

'Yes?'

'Your dinner's spoiling. Come and eat.'

'Coming,' he yelled down the stairs, adding quietly, 'in a minute.'

He was lost. He had wandered into a maze in the tunnels. He turned left. A blank wall. He retraced his steps. He recognised the same pattern of openings and blind alleys that he had seen often before. He could walk around but he was trapped in a prison. The Driller, wherever he was, was getting further and further away. George Hacker jabbed sore fingers on the keys of the computer, his anger making him forget where he had just come from, so that when he turned the next corner he saw that he was, once again, back where he had started.

'Sorry,' he whispered, as though the children could hear him. 'I'm sorry, but I'm stuck. I can't get out.'

He turned and turned, tried every trick he could think of. He tried turning right every time. He came to a dead end. He tried turning left every time. It led him in a huge circle back to his starting point. His ears began to buzz with tiredness and annoyance. He wiped his sleeve across his eyes to try to clear them and was surprised to see that it came away from his face wet with tears. He slumped back in his chair, resting his hands on the edge of the desk. His fingers were trembling, not just with fatigue, but with fear for the children if they should meet the Driller before he did.

He leaned forward, screwed up his face and stared at the screen.

'Perhaps,' he said, 'if I just go backwards instead of straight on.' He moved the cursor cautiously.

'No,' she said firmly, with much more confidence than she really felt. 'We're going to ask for help. It'll be all right.'

'Please.'

'Come on.' She strode towards the tent, half dragging him after her.

'You will tell us.' Ali's voice shrieked angrily. 'What did they do then?'

Wendy pushed at the flap. It seemed rude to just walk in but of course there was no bell to ring or door to knock at. A shaft of light from inside lashed diagonally across her face.

'Where are they? Where did they – ' Ali began.

Wendy and Matthew stepped into the tent.

'I'm sorry,' apologised Wendy. 'I know it's very rude.'

Ali stopped in astonishment. 'What?'

Amina gaped.

'Here.' Rahila smiled. 'They're here. It will tell itself now.'

Looter was surprised that someone as thin as Hardly could be so heavy. They staggered along, blind at the end of the dismal procession through the dark tunnels. Looter had his hand around Hardly propping him up. The light from the uplifted wand barely penetrated the dark where they were. Hardly tripped, twisted his ankle and dragged himself from Looter's grip. He leaned against the wall and groaned.

'Can't do it.'

'Yes, you can.' Looter knew it was not true. Hardly could not go any further and he could not carry him any more.

'No.'

'Stop!' yelled Looter.

'What's up?' called Colin.

'Wait a bit.'

Samneric held hands and kept silent.

'Mustn't wait,' said James.

'We'll have to,' said Peter. 'We can't leave him here.'

They clustered around Hardly. He was glad to be in a stronger light now that James was near to him. It cheered him.

'Get away from the wall,' Peter advised. 'It's slimy.'

''Snot,' said Bins.

Looter smacked him. 'Don't say that. Hardly's tired.'

'Ow!' yelled Bins. 'Don't! I didn't. I mean it's not slimy. Look.' He dragged his hand down the wall and showed them his palm. It was dusty.

They looked around. In their exhaustion and determined advance the boys had stopped noticing the tunnels. Now they saw that they were clean and dry. They sniffed. Did the air still stink?

'Better?' asked Peter.

Looter took a deep breath. 'Yes. A bit. I can go on a bit more.'

They formed again into their procession, this time with

Hardly towards the front, nearer the light. A few paces took them to a left-hand turn. James went round the corner, then stopped. Bins walked into Colin. His spectacles dislodged themselves and skewed round on his nose.

'What's up?'

'Oh no.' James groaned.

'What?' They crushed forward to peer round the corner.

'Dead end,' Peter announced. 'Got to turn round.'

'Why?'

'Where?'

'Wherever the wand leads us.'

'But it brought us here.'

James turned to go back. The light snapped off. He faced the blank wall and the light came on again.

'Can't go back,' he said.


'Oh, I'm so glad,' Wendy said when they had explained their sudden entrance. The royal children made them welcome. 'We were so frightened to walk in.'

'We'll look after you,' Ali promised grandly.

Amina danced round, kicking cushions.

'It's so exciting,' she squealed. 'And a happy ending. You see.' She pointed a finger at Ali. 'The happiest ending ever.'

Matthew pushed a pile of cushions together to make a little nest and he curled up in it like a harvest mouse in hay.

'Wendy,' said Rahila. 'It is a funny name.' She smoothed her long hair. 'You are a princess too?'

Wendy smiled. 'No. Only to my father.'

Ali insisted. 'But yes. Look at you. Your fine robes. Certainly a princess.'

'Just someone who's tired and needs some help.' She laughed nervously. Ali brandished his sword.

'So easy,' he said, 'to help you.'

'What a wonderful thing,' Amina cried.

The tent flap stirred. The horses' low whinnying switched to a high scream. The light in the tent grew dim as a shadow passed over the lamp. Ali flicked his head from side to side trying to see where the harsh jangling came from.

'Look.' Amina pointed to a bundle of sparks.

Rahila screamed at what she saw next.

A tall figure leaped into the tent, red hair aglow, a fearful scar disfiguring his cruel face. A drill screamed and twisted at his wrist. His mouth opened in a yell, showing the pointed steel teeth.

'Yahoo!'

He swept Ali's sword to one side. Tink flew straight into Rahila's face, making her lose her balance and topple over on to Matthew. The shadow pounced on top of Wendy. It could not hold her or beat her but the touch of its cold anger made her feel sick and dizzy.

'Gotcha,' crowed the Driller. 'Yahoo!'

A pain stabbed into her side.

'Oh,' she moaned. 'Pain. Pain. Peter.'

'My arms ache,' James complained.

'Put it down for a bit,' said Peter. 'We'll sit in the dark.'

'No,' said Eric, or it might have been Sam. 'Not the dark.'

'It's not like that,' said James. 'I can't. I'm not holding it up. I'm dragging it down.'

'Let's see.'

James relaxed his grip and the wand carried his arms higher. It banged on the cave roof. A shower of earth scattered down.

'See?'

'Let it do it again.'

James pulled the wand down and it flew back up. More of the ceiling dislodged.

'Again.'

More.

'Again.'

The whole roof of the tunnel was burying the boys. Earth first, mixed with rock, then sand, then warm ash from a recent fire.

'Look,' yelled Peter.

The boys, standing in a circle, raised their heads. Cool air played over their faces. Above them the black sky was shot through with stars. Peter crowed and flew up into the air. He dropped back down, put an arm round Looter and another round Hardly and lifted them up. James took Bins and Colin. Samneric tried to scramble up the side but they kept slipping back. Peter dropped back down for them. They stood, feet sinking into the sand, at the edge of a dead fire pit.

Peter thumped James on the back. 'We made it. We made it!' James grinned and grinned and screwed his wand into the sand. The Lost Boys shook hands with each other and kicked the sand in delight. Bins took off his specs and dragged his arm across wet eyes.

A screen pierced the air. Then a terrible yell.

'Yahoo!'

The boys froze. Peter moved first. He flew to the tent. James was second, dragging his wand from the sand.

Mrs Hacker shook George's shoulders.

'Come and eat,' she said angrily. 'Stop playing with that stupid game.'

'Hey,' he yelled. His fingers slipped from the controls and stabbed wildly at the keyboard. 'You've spoiled it.'

'Eat,' she shouted. 'Eat! Stop wasting your time.'

The screen flickered and flashed. The tunnels disappeared.

> CODE BROKEN
> ESCAPE
> EXTRA 10,000 POINTS

A bleeper whooped out his accidental success. When the confusion cleared, his cursor was by a lakeside with palm trees, tents, horses and camels.

'Hello,' said George. 'Where do we go now?'

He edged the cursor towards a tent.

The Driller reached his hand out and grabbed Wendy's wailing throat. He pointed the drill at her head.

'Yahoo!'

The drill squealed.

'Do it!' yelled Tink. 'Do it!'

'Shut up.'

'What?' she jangled.

'I said shut up,' Peter repeated.

The Driller snarled and swivelled his head around, taking his attention from Wendy. Ali grabbed his scimitar and swung it, hitting the Driller on the back of his legs. He screamed, dropped Wendy and faced Peter and Ali. Blood oozed down the back of his legs.

Peter, dagger drawn, threw back his head and crowed. The shadow fell on him and he was instantly silent, the roar of triumph choked in his throat. He doubled up in pain, grabbing at his side. Tink jangled derisively.

'All over. All over,' she cackled.

Ali quaked as he stood alone against the Driller. Rahila bundled Amina and Matthew under a huge pile of rugs and cushions to hide them.

'Then he came in,' she whispered to herself. 'Wand held high.'

Then he came in, wand held high. His wizard's robe was black as the night sky and the pattern of stars glowed with a separate life.

'Boys with sticks,' laughed the Driller. 'And girls.' He laughed again. 'All over. All over. Yahoo!'

George drove the cursor on into the tent. At last: the Driller. He pushed the 'fire' button.

James lowered his staff and pointed it at the Driller.

'All over,' he commanded.

The drill squealed louder than ever. The Driller's face contorted with terror and he began to spin like the drill. Faster and faster. He became a blur, then a grey light. Then, with a final and frenzied wail, he disappeared.

GAME OVER
YOU WIN

'Ha!' shouted George. 'Done it! Got him!'

Peter lay dazed. He blinked, seeing nothing. Wendy rubbed her hand cautiously over her throat where the Driller had grabbed her. She knelt by his side, stooped and kissed his forehead. He smiled.

'Pain?' she asked.

'Sort of.'

'Where?'

He rubbed his side. 'Not here any more. Not sure where. All over?'

'Yes.'

He stood uncertainly. His shadow fell obediently away from the light.

Tink whizzed across the tent and back again, over and over, so fast it made their heads spin to look at her. She was beside herself with fury. She flew directly at Wendy, slapped against her face and shot out of the tent.

'Where's she off to?' asked Colin.

'Dunno,' said Peter. 'They're like that. They come and go. There'll be another.'

'Looter!' shouted Matthew. His head was poking out of the pile of rugs and he saw the Lost Boys step into the tent. He ran across and flung himself at the boy. Looter hugged him gladly.

'Hello, Wendy,' whispered Bins. She squeezed his arm. His face turned pink and the lens in his spectacles misted up.

'Welcome,' said Ali to Colin and Hardly, leading them over to places of honour by the stove. Samneric dived for the rugs and burrowed under.

'Is it a happy ending?' asked Amina.

'Nearly,' Rahila assured her. 'Nearly happy. Nearly ended.'

George tossed the Driller software into the waste bin in the kitchen.

'Will they be all right?' asked his wife.

He sat down to eat his dinner.

'Yes,' he said. 'Yes. I think they will.'

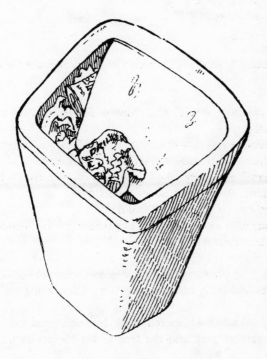

# Fourteen

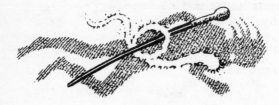

'CAN'T you stay?' asked Ali.

'I'm sorry,' said Wendy. 'We'd love to, but we can't.'

'Do you really fly?' asked Amina.

'Yes,' shouted Matthew, and he leaped up and soared around.

'They do,' said Wendy. 'I can't any more.'

'Then how will you get home?' asked Rahila.

'I don't know. But I think we've got to go back to the beach and Pirate's Cove. After all, that's where we arrived.'

'Yes.'

The three royal children watched them disappear into the fire pit and back into the tunnels that led deep beneath the lake.

'That was a wonderful story,' said Amina.

'Thank you.'

'What will the next one be about?' asked Ali.

'I don't think I'm going to tell any more.'

'Are you going to leave us?' Bins asked.

'I suppose so. If I can get home.'

'Do you want to go home?'

'Yes.'

'Oh.'

'Do you?' she asked him.

'Got no home,' he said quietly.

'We're Lost,' said Sam, or it might have been Eric.

'Couldn't fly back anyway,' said Hardly.

'Keep going,' ordered Peter, who did not like the way the conversation was going.

'These tunnels really aren't so bad,' said Wendy.

'They get worse,' Peter assured her. 'Smelly.'

'And wet,' said Bins.

'And slimy,' added Hardly.

'And you wait till you see the nightmares,' warned Colin. 'All dead in the path.'

But there were no dead nightmares, and the way remained clean and clear and the path easy.

'Are you sure?' asked Peter. 'It doesn't seem right.'

'Nothing to do with me,' said James. 'I just go where the wand leads me.'

'I thought they were caves,' said Wendy.

'They are.'

'No. It's not rock.'

They stopped. James held the wand high. The tunnel was a perfect arch of red bricks.

'It can't be,' said Peter.

'Just look.'

They rubbed it with their hands. Under their feet, instead of the jagged rock floor there were slabs of laid stone.

'We're going the wrong way,' Peter insisted.

'I don't mind,' said Hardly. 'I don't want to go back into those caves.'

'No,' agreed Eric, or it might have been Sam.

'There are still trolls in there,' said Sam, or it might have been Eric.

They walked on. There were rats sometimes. Wendy and Matthew did not like that but the others had seen so many nightmares in the other tunnels that they just laughed at the furry brown bodies and shiny tails.

A brick fell from the roof behind them.

'It's a bit crumbly,' said Colin.

'All the cement's loose.' Matthew prodded at some mortar with his finger and it dribbled out. A split in the brickwork widened, crawled up the arch and over their heads.

'Move on. Quickly,' Peter ordered.

'Not again.' said James.

'What?'

They faced a brick wall. Behind them the tunnel was caving in with a menacing booming.

'Smash it,' said Peter. 'With the wand.'

Dust choked their throats. It stung their eyes. James bashed the end of his wand against the wall like a battering ram. It fell through and the boys and Wendy dived and scrambled to safety just as the whole tunnel collapsed.

'We'll never get back that way,' said Eric.

'No,' agreed Sam.

'Give us some light,' said Peter.

James held up the wand. Nothing happened.

'Come on,' Bins complained. 'I don't like it in the dark.'

'Nothing's happening,' said James. 'I can't make it work.'

Above them, in the dark, a door creaked open.

'Drink?' asked Mrs Hacker.

'Mmmm?' He was drowsy.

'Whiskey?'

'Oh. Yes, please.'

She put a glass by his arm and reached out to him. He hugged her.

'Please let them come back,' she said.

'They will.'

'I got them something.'

'Mmmm?'

Mrs Hacker brought in a carrier bag. He took it from her and unwrapped the packages.

'Shoes?'

'Yes.'

'Why?'

'It's the new ones they wanted. The day they left. The ones I said they couldn't have.' She blew her nose vigorously.

'Good.' He took a sip of his whiskey.

'George?'

He put an arm round her.

'Don't. It'll be all right.' He put the shoes to his nose to draw in the fragrance of the new leather. 'What on earth?' He leaped from his chair, knocking his drink over. A booming echo rose up from deep beneath them.

'Sounds like a bomb.'

'No,' he said. 'It was in the house.'

'The cellar?'

'I think so.'

They went to the hall. Puffs of dust were floating under the cellar door.

'Stay back.'

He strode over and flung open the door, snapped the light switch on. Ten very dirty faces peered up at him, one through the single lens of a broken pair of spectacles.

'Hello, Dad,' said James.

'We're back,' said Wendy.

'Mummy! Mummy!' Matthew squeaked.

Mrs Hacker pushed past her husband and stared down.

'Oh,' she said. 'Ooooh.'

'Hello, chaps,' said Mr Hacker. 'Good to see you.'

They ate all the packets of breakfast cereal. They crammed toast into their mouths. They drank all the milk in the house.

'Can I have muesli, please?' said Matthew. 'I'd rather.'

'Course you can,' said George. 'Whatever.' He hugged him for about the ninetieth time.

Matthew squeezed his father and put his lips up to whisper in his ear. 'Trolls do stink,' he said.

'Do they?' his father asked. 'Perhaps you'll tell me all about it soon.'

'Yes, please,' said Matthew.

They took baths two at a time, except for Hardly who fitted in with Sam and Eric, and Wendy who had hers on her own. George and Mrs Hacker tidied the kitchen and washed up in a daze while the children looked for pyjamas, tracksuits, spare shirts, anything they could sleep in. When they were dressed they held a secret conference. They made their decision and elected James spokesperson. Then they went downstairs again.

'They want to stay,' James proposed. 'Can they?'

George and his wife looked at each other. He counted. 'Seven. Plus you three. That's ten.'

'Nine,' said Peter. He was still wearing the skeleton leaves James had discovered him in.

'Peter's going back,' said James. 'Nine.'

Mrs Hacker stepped over to him and took his hand. 'Don't you think it's time to stay?' she asked. She stroked his hair.

'Please stay,' urged Wendy.

Mrs Hacker tried to put her arm around him but he pulled away.

'Got to get back.'

'Can you fly all that way?' asked Mrs Hacker. 'You look . . . older.'

'It's the first time you've seen him,' James protested.

'Oh no,' she said.

'No,' agreed Peter. 'I'll get back.' He furrowed his brow. Mrs Hacker leaned forward and kissed him lightly. He brightened.

'Thimbles,' he said. 'Time to go.' He turned and bounded up the stairs.

Mrs Hacker raced after him. She was too late. The breeze lifted the curtain from the open window. She saw a shadow against the moon.

'Goodbye,' she shouted. 'Goodbye, Peter.'

He turned, lifted a hand to wave, threw back his head to crow goodbye and sped on.

'Second to the right,' she said quietly. 'And straight on till morning.'

Dawn was breaking over the Neverland. Peter flew first to the eastern shore of the cove. The bangs and clattering were louder than ever from beyond the trees. He swooped low over the jungle and past the cove. In the next bay bulldozers were clearing the ground. Cement mixers spun furiously. Cranes lifted piles of bricks to the tops of scaffolding towers. The glass and concrete blocks of the hotels were drawing closer. The rubbish vans dumped new piles of burger boxes and chip papers into the tip. He frowned, banked round and headed back to Pirate's Cove.

The gentle rippling of the water was broken by the forlorn strokes of the crocodile as it set off towards the wrecked galleon. As Peter reappeared the tide turned with a sudden force and the ship creaked out a last death rattle. The spurs and struts groaned away from their rotten joints, heaved into the waves and were carried out to the open sea. The crocodile stopped, Peter hovered above. Together, with an uncertain memory of what the ship had been, they watched the flotsam disappear for ever. The crocodile turned and paddled back to the jungle. Peter scanned the beach. He waited.

'Not today,' he said at last.

Just then the foliage shifted and a single figure broke through the jungle's edge and wandered on to the beach. It looked around, lonely, Lost.

'That's it,' smiled Peter. He darted to the shore.


'I really don't know,' complained George. 'It'll have to be bunks.' He settled James in his room with Colin, Hardly and Bins.

'Couldn't I go with Wendy?' Bins pleaded.

'I don't think so, old son,' he apologised.

James took his staff to the corner of the room. It felt very light now. He gripped it with both hands and placed his feet apart.

'What are you doing?' asked his father.

'Oh, nothing,' said James. And he wasn't. Sadly, he leaned the stick in the corner and climbed into bed.

Sam and Eric and Looter were in Matthew's room.

'There's the computer,' said Matthew. 'I'll show it to you in the morning.'

Looter smiled.

Mrs Hacker sat on Wendy's bed.

'So you knew him, too?' said Wendy.

'Oh yes.'

'Will he come back?'

'For you?'

'Yes.'

'I don't think so.'

'No,' agreed Wendy.

Mrs Hacker stooped to kiss her.

'Does everyone know him? Peter Pain?'

'Peter?'

The next book in Toby Forward's enthralling **Neverland** series is **The Book of Lies**.